Unschoolers

Unschoolers

Sophia Sayigh & Milva McDonald

Library of Congress Control Number: 2017900858
Published in the United States by Sophia Sayigh, Arlington, MA

ISBN 978-0-9985894-0-4
ISBN 978-0-9985894-2-8 (ebook edition)

Printed in the United States of America

First Printing, 2017

unschoolersbook.com

Cover design: Julie Nathon Sayigh
Cover photo: NASA

Carry a candle in the dark, be a candle in the dark, know that you're a flame in the dark.

—IVAN ILLICH

Contents

Home Learning Together Directory

Parent 1	Parent 2	Child(ren): Name & age
Pina Morelli	Lou Morelli	Anthony 15, Dominic 12, Aria 10 Morelli
Teresa (Reesie) Ellstrom	Russell Hornick	Otto 14, Vera 11, Romeo 8 Hornick
Carmen García	Henry Wells	Elizabeth (Lizzie) 12, Anne 10, Emma 7 Wells
Jewel Swanson	Chuck Swanson	Sky 11, Joy 9, Rock 6, Blue 3 Swanson
Sam Falk	Stacy Parsons	Tyler 8, Jasper 7 Falk-Parsons
Priscilla Lieberman	Ron Lieberman	Felix 7, Gabby 5 Lieberman
Melissa Wright	Gary Bennison	Zoe 13, Jacob 10 Bennison-Wright
Ellen Rutherford		Cora 13 Lee
Nasim Abbas	Sarah Abbas	Tarek 9 Abbas
Alice Stiles	Bill Stiles	Isaac 12, Willy 10, Lucy 6, Tuck 2, Silas 6 mos. Stiles

No Vacation for Homeschoolers

By Frankie Reynolds
Special to The Sun

Posted June 6, 2015 at 12:51 PM

Anthony Morelli's chemistry final is behind him, his book group is winding down, and he's looking forward to spending time playing his bass this summer. He's not waiting for the end of school, though. The fifteen-year-old homeschools, and like the growing number of homeschoolers throughout the nation, his education runs on a different clock.

"Some things end for the summer, but some keep going," said the teenager in a conversation at his home. "Chemistry and book group end, and I have a month or two off from bass lessons, but that doesn't mean I stop playing." His summer will also be spent in band practice with his friends, and continuing his volunteer position with the live animal program at Kaufman Nature Center.

"We stay active," said mom Pina Morelli, who organizes a book club for homeschoolers and is one of the leaders of Home Learning Together (HoLT), a local homeschooling support group. "The together part really describes what we do," she said. "We're a busy

3

bunch. But the founders also chose the name for the acronym, which honors John Holt."

Holt, who died in 1985, was a proponent of homeschooling, and coined the term "unschooling." "Holt really meant the term to describe learning that happens outside school," said Morelli. "It also means we don't replicate school. The kids lead the way, and they're learning all the time," she said, echoing the title of one of Holt's books.

Homeschooling moms Teresa Ellstrom and Carmen García concur.

On a recent sunny Wednesday at Willow Park, Ellstrom and García were among the parents standing by while kids engaged in various activities including an organized game of Ultimate Frisbee. "Learning isn't limited to certain activities, or to home," said García. "It's constant."

"Think about babies and toddlers," said Ellstrom. "People are wired to learn. You don't have to force them."

"I've been to school and I've homeschooled," said thirteen-year-old Zoe Bennison-Wright, whose interests include poetry, neuroscience, and editing her homegrown literary journal, *Acorn*. "For me, there's no question. I prefer homeschooling."

According to Ellstrom, homeschooled kids have more freedom to pursue their goals, which can include entrepreneurship. Ellstrom's teenage son Otto likes music and computers, and recently hung out his shingle to teach budding guitar players. "I have three students so far," he said. "I hope to have more next year."

What about socialization? "Look around," said García, gesturing to the clusters of children and teens at the park. "Obviously, it's not an issue."

Ellstrom agreed. "A lot of people homeschool because they don't like the interactions their kids are experiencing in school."

What about college? "My oldest is fourteen," said Ellstrom, "so we've talked about it some, but there's plenty of time."

"Colleges like homeschoolers because they tend to be motivated, and focused on learning. That makes a huge difference," said García, adding that homeschoolers have gained admission to colleges across the country.

According to Ellstrom, academics, socialization, and standing out on college admissions are all great, but they're not what keeps her going. "We love the lifestyle," she said. "Learning out in the world, building strong relationships, and really, just enjoying every day. It's living the good life."

HoLT members are looking forward to their annual June gathering at Ellstrom's house. "It's become one of our homeschooling traditions," she said.

CHAPTER 1

Jewel

Monday, June 10

JEWEL woke early, before any of her kids, which was saying a lot. Sky, on the cusp of adolescence, had started to languish in bed later than she used to, but the younger three got up practically with the dawn.

"Come on, baby, stay in bed," Chuck urged, snuggling into her. As warm and inviting as he felt, she declined his offer. Her yoga practice demanded it. "You know what you're missing, don't you?" crooned her groggy husband as she pulled on her yoga pants.

"I'm not missing anything," she said, giving his shoulder a squeeze. "It'll be available later."

Chuck laughed. "Not tonight, or tomorrow night," he said. "I won't be here. But I'm talking about Blue."

"What about him?" Jewel answered through the pink cotton T-shirt she was slipping over her head.

"In the morning he hops in bed, kisses me, and says, 'Sun's up!'"

"I know," said Jewel, grabbing a towel.

"You should stay for it," said Chuck.

She kissed him. "Not today," she said, and left.

IT WAS cool in the yoga corner, and by the time she finished, bright. Their house was small for a family of six, but she'd carved out this space for herself and defended it fiercely. Her kids gave her a hard time about a lot of things, but not this. Even Rock knew that his mother's yoga corner was sacred.

As Jewel wiped the sweat from her brow and took one last cleansing breath, she heard a hubbub from the kitchen. It sounded like unhappy voices, not something she wanted to hear on a beautiful day. The kids needed to get their work done if they wanted to get outdoors. Jewel hoped they would oblige, because she really wanted to spend some time in the sunshine.

A sharp, high-pitched voice yelled "No, Blue!" It was Rock, as usual. Jewel hated the way he clashed with his younger brother. She had tried long talks, peaceful sibling workshops, and more time-outs than she could count, but nothing worked. The two boys were like oil and water.

As she opened the door to the kitchen, willing herself to maintain the calm she'd just achieved, she heard their bickering loud and clear. She entered the kitchen and there they were, engaged in a tug of war with a yogurt tube, Rock's shrill voice shooting holes in her hard-earned morning peace. "It's mine!"

"Stop it, boys!" Jewel demanded. By the time she got to them, the tube had burst, and blueberry yogurt was splattered on their hands and Blue's arms and face.

"Uh oh," said Joy, who was seated at the kitchen table eating a bowl of homemade granola.

Blue let out a wail and Jewel lifted him into her arms, grabbing a kitchen towel to wipe him off. "Time out!" she yelled to Rock.

"But, Mom," he complained, "I had it first."

"You're older and you know better," she said, pointing to the time-out chair.

Rock stalked over to it and sat with his back to them. His scrunched posture made no bones about his feelings on the matter. She'd talk to him, but first she had to deal with her screaming kid.

"It's OK, honey," she said, kissing the yogurt off Blue's face. "Mmmm, yummy!" That made him laugh. She did it again and in no time he'd forgotten his troubles. "Now, little Blue," she said, opening the refrigerator and finding the last box of yogurt tubes hidden behind the tub of organic spring mix she'd bought yesterday. "How about some yogurt?"

"Oh, yes," he cried happily. "Nummy!" That had been Blue's word for the breast when she was nursing him, and now it was his word for yogurt. Jewel wondered what that said about the taste of her milk.

She tore the tube open, handed it to him, and seated him next to Joy on the bench. "Hi buddy," Joy said, snuggling next to him. Blue smiled and Joy tickled his tummy, making him laugh and squirm.

"None of that while he's eating," said Jewel. She didn't want any more mess. Joy obliged. She was Jewel's easiest child, but then again, Sky used to be simple, too, until she hit double digits. Jewel couldn't help but think that part of the problem was Vera and Dominic and Anne and the other homeschoolers Sky liked to socialize with. She had figured out that their parents didn't require them to do school work. Jewel had talked to Teresa about it some, but as much as Jewel wanted to keep an open mind, she couldn't wrap her head around letting her kids direct their own learning. Besides, Chuck let the kids run the roost whenever he was around. Somebody had to keep order, and for better or worse, that somebody was her.

With Blue and Joy happily situated and eating breakfast, it was time to deal with Rock.

His body was still folded tightly in dismay, small shoulders drooping, arms crossed, head lowered. Jewel knelt in front of the time-out chair. "Honey?" she whispered. He didn't move or answer. "Rock, look at me."

"I want Daddy," he whispered.

"He's at work," Jewel said. Chuck had left for the fire station early, not long after she started doing yoga. He'd come in to give her a quick kiss, lying on his back to gain access to her lips while she was in downward dog.

Jewel ruffled Rock's wild curls and placed her hand under his chin to draw his face up. He obliged, barely, revealing eyes that were squinched shut. "Come on, bud," she said. "Look at me." When he finally did, Jewel saw that his closed eyes were an attempt to contain his tears. She stroked his hair, wrapping thick, tangled ringlets around her fingers. "I can't have this fighting all the time," she said.

A scoff came from Sky, who'd just shuffled into the kitchen in her pajamas. "But you do," she said, opening the breakfast cabinet. "You *do* have it all the time."

"That's enough, Sky," said Jewel. "Why aren't you dressed?"

"I just got up," she said, pouring granola into a bowl.

"Well, you're already behind," said Jewel. "Get to work so we can enjoy the day. We're supposed to meet Teresa and Pina and maybe some others for a walk this afternoon."

"Is Vera going?" Sky liked all the kids, but Teresa's daughter was her best friend. If anything would make her get her work done, it would be the opportunity to be with her.

"Yes," said Jewel, lamenting that Sky's motivation came from her social life, but also feeling grateful that it meant she'd have less of a struggle getting her to comply.

Jewel turned back to Rock. "Want some yogurt now?" she said. He nodded, still fighting to swallow the tears. "OK," she said and lifted him up, something she rarely did anymore. His grasp surprised her. He pressed his face into her shoulder and wrapped his arms and legs around her like a giant snake. "Hey," she said softly, "a little looser, honey, OK?"

As usual, he didn't listen, just held on like his life depended on it.

SKY, still in her PJs, climbed into the bottom bunk. Joy was with the boys in the work 'n' play area (Jewel's name for the finished basement) but she could come in at any moment, so Sky pulled the makeshift curtain she'd set up to try and give herself some privacy. It was just a blanket, but it did the trick. She squeezed herself into the corner in the relative darkness and flipped open her laptop. Thank goodness for her cousins. If they didn't get rid of stuff so often, Sky might not have a computer at all.

All she really wanted to do was watch—again—the movie of *Romeo and Juliet* she'd taken out of the library the day before. The librarian had helped her order two other versions from different libraries, one another movie, and one a recording of a live performance filmed in London. He had also shown her where to find some more Shakespeare plays to read. Anne said Elizabeth liked *Twelfth Night* so she figured she'd read that one first.

It would all have to wait, because she had to produce a book report before they'd be able to leave the house, and she really wanted to go on that nature walk. She hadn't seen Vera in a while and she needed to talk to her about the *Romeo and Juliet* movie, and *Matilda,* which Vera had recommended to her. Sky loved it, which would make the book report a lot easier to write. It was loads better than the last book she'd read, one of those dumb *American Girl* things her mother insisted on.

At the family meeting last week, Sky had argued that she should be able to choose all of her own books from now on. When her mother said she needed to read at least some educational books, her dad remarked that there wasn't much to worry about if Shakespeare was on the list, at which point her mother gave in, reluctantly. It was a big victory. Next up was getting them to let her decide on her own writing projects. Instead of doing book reports and synopses of history chapters, she'd write movie reviews. Maybe Zoe would even put one of them in *Acorn*.

Thankfully, things had quieted down since the yogurt disaster at breakfast, so Sky didn't need to put in her earplugs. They didn't work very well, anyway. When Rock and Blue got going, nothing could block out the noise. She opened a blank document and started writing. "Matilda is a very powerful girl. Even though she has special powers like moving things with her mind, a trick called telekinesis, her real power comes from her smarts."

She was on paragraph four and about to wrap the whole thing up when she heard Joy's footsteps. "Sky," she sang. "Oh, Sky."

Joy pulled the blanket aside and Sky closed her laptop. "I told you a million times to say knock knock before you open my curtain."

"Oh, yeah," said Joy, tapping on the wooden headboard.

Sky scooted herself to the edge of the bed and stood up. "It's too late, silly, you already opened it."

"Did you do your book report?" asked Joy, hugging her Hello Kitty lunchbox, another acquisition from the cousins. A smear of peanut butter covered Hello Kitty's red bow, and the end of a yellow banana stuck out from the zipper pocket.

"Nope," said Sky. "Sorry."

Joy wagged a finger at her sister. "But then we can't go out!"

"If you want to go out, get out of here so I can do it."

"I'm getting Mom," said Joy.

"Go for it," yelled Sky as Joy bolted. She rummaged through her drawer, pulled out a pair of jeans and her favorite green shirt, and got dressed.

ELEVEN a.m. came and went, and they were still in the house.

"Mom, can't we go out?"

Jewel finished rinsing the lentils she was sprouting and hugged Joy. "I'm sorry, honey. I want to go out, too, but Sky and Rock are still working."

"But I finished everything!" Joy's voice rang with accusations of injustice.

Jewel understood her feelings, but she couldn't just let her other kids off the hook. She took Joy's hand. "Let's see how everyone else is doing."

They walked downstairs to the work 'n' play area, and found Rock and Blue sitting in the corner building with Legos. Although Rock should have been doing math, it was nice to see them playing together. "Rock," said Jewel. "I hope you're done with your work." She looked on the table and saw that he'd only half completed his work sheets. "Nope," she said.

Joy stamped her foot. "That means it's even longer until we can go out."

"Wait," said Rock. "I stopped because I didn't know an answer."

Rock and Joy were heading toward meltdown status. Jewel felt like she might be getting there herself. She closed her eyes and silently counted to ten, then said, "Rock, let's sit down and finish this together. Joy, find out how Sky is doing."

"I just did," said Joy, "and she wasn't finished."

"Well, check again while I help Rock."

Jewel and Rock had only gotten through two questions, which he had absolutely no trouble with, when she heard Joy and Sky going at it. Eight more questions, just eight more and Rock's work would be finished for the day. "Honey," she said. "You seem to be doing fine. Do the rest of these so we can go out, OK?"

He nodded his head, and she headed up to Joy and Sky's room. "Here," said Sky, handing Jewel her laptop with the screen showing her book report on *Matilda*.

Jewel gave it a quick skim. "This looks great," she said. She might have given it a closer look, but Sky's writing was pretty advanced. "Once Rock is finished, we can go."

Joy scowled at her sister. "You said you didn't do it."

Sky laughed. "I was just kidding. I didn't want to do it, believe me."

Jewel headed back to the basement and breathed a sigh of relief when she saw that Rock had completed the work sheet, apparently in no time at all.

Why the heck did they insist on being so resistant? She had no answer, she only knew it exhausted her. She wished she had someone to talk to about it. Teresa would listen, but she wouldn't get it. Forget Pina, she'd have plenty of opinions and wouldn't hesitate to express them. Nasim only had one kid to worry about, she hardly saw Alice, and Carmen's kids were perfect. She used to be able to vent to Sam, but then Sam started telling her how much easier life had gotten since they'd lightened up on the school at home thing, and Jewel didn't want to hear that. Maybe someday she'd get there, but for now, it wasn't happening. She knew Melissa understood, but she seemed to have so little time to get together, and who was Jewel kidding, she didn't have the time, either.

Still, she felt like she needed an outing with friends more than her kids did. Thank goodness they had finished in time—just in time—to join the others for the walk. "Come on troops," she said, scooping up Blue and grabbing the snack bag she'd packed earlier. "Let's go."

She felt the tension drain from her as they stepped outside together. "Yay!" said Joy, doing a happy dance. Rock joined her. Even Sky had shed her pre-adolescent scowl. Jewel took a moment to breathe in the fresh air before they piled into the minivan.

JEWEL had to drive fast to get to the state park in time to meet everyone. The group was just leaving, walking toward the head of the trail when she pulled into the parking lot. She and the kids emerged from the van quickly.

They were all laughing as they ran, Rock calling "Tyler! Jasper! Wait for me!"

Teresa turned around and saw them, and called for everyone to stop so they had a chance to catch up. Romeo barked as they approached. "O Romeo, Romeo, wherefore art thou, Romeo?" Sky crooned when she saw him. Jewel couldn't understand why, but her daughter loved that dog almost as much as Teresa did. Teresa took him everywhere, and nuzzled and kissed him like he was a baby. Jewel theorized that Teresa had actually gotten the dog instead of having another baby, but Jewel thought it was a poor substitute.

Romeo snorted as Sky scratched his jowls, his pink tongue hanging loosely out of his mouth as he panted. Sky laughed and said, "Oh, speak again bright angel!"

Vera and Teresa had invited Sky to see a production of *Romeo and Juliet* with them, and Sky had loved it. Afterward, she told Jewel to get her a copy of the play. She'd been spouting lines from it ever since.

"Hi, Jewel!" Teresa gave her a hug, as did Pina. Sam was busy talking to the little boys.

"OK," said Teresa, moving forward. "We're off!"

Walking in the quiet woods under a canopy of trees, breathing the fresh air, and being with friends felt like bliss. "I wish I did this every day," said Jewel, hands free except for a shoulder bag filled with water, snacks, and her travel first aid kit. Blue was between Sky and Vera, holding each of their hands, content as could be. Joy and Aria and Tyler were on some kind of wildflower hunt, taking inventory of the number and varieties they found along the path. Rock and Jasper had already found two caterpillars and were on the hunt for more.

"You could be doing it every day," said Pina. "If you forgot about those work sheets."

Pina had said it with a smile, as though it were nothing more than a friendly suggestion, but still, Jewel felt her cheeks get hot. "Don't start," she said.

Teresa put an arm around Jewel and squeezed her shoulder. "Are you coming to Presentation Night?"

"We're planning on it," said Jewel. She never liked to promise, because sometimes she had to say no to plans, but she hoped it would work out. She had a presentation of her own she wanted to do.

Teresa stayed quiet, but Pina, as usual, piped in. "That's not a yes," she said. "It's Presentation Night. Just give them the day off."

"I'll think about it," said Jewel. Really, she just wanted Pina to shut up. They'd already hashed through this more than once, because there had been times when Joy hadn't finished her school work or chores and Jewel, at the last minute, had to cancel plans with Aria. Pina had been happy to share her opinion about that.

Teresa, thankfully, changed the subject. "Are your kids presenting?" she said.

"Yes," said Jewel.

"What are they doing?" asked Pina, and Jewel cringed. The answer to that question would bring them right back to the uncomfortable conversation they'd just left.

Teresa came to the rescue again. "It will be nice to see Chuck," she said. "He's coming, right?"

"Yes," said Jewel. Fortunately, Presentation Night was on one of his off days.

They came to a clearing and found Sam, who had gone ahead with Jasper and Rock. Blue let go of Sky and Vera's hands and bounded into the tall grass. Aria and Joy headed for a patch of purple flowers, pencil and paper in hand. Rock, his fist full of the pebbles he'd collected while hunting caterpillars, ran to meet Jewel and with his free hand, pulled at her bag. She gave him a

Tupperware filled with carrot and celery sticks in exchange for the pebbles, which she stowed away in the bag's outer pocket. Rock skipped to Tyler and Jasper, who were already eating crackers and hummus.

Teresa and Pina and Sam sat on a rock, talking, and Sky and Vera joined them. Jewel did, too, soaking up the sun's warmth like manna from heaven.

CHAPTER 2

Priscilla

Tuesday, June 11

FELIX and Gabby sat in front of the television while Priscilla cooked. She washed and dried her hands, dumped some almond meal in a bowl, seasoned it with salt and pepper, then cracked two eggs into another bowl and stirred them with a fork.

As her hand methodically spun in circles, Priscilla took a deep breath and closed her eyes. The kids were so quiet when they watched TV. The women in her preschool moms group spoke often and effusively of the electronic babysitter. It was something they laughed about and bonded over, except for Priscilla.

She understood what they meant, especially at moments like this. After a long day, cocooned in the kitchen while the early summer air wafted into newly opened windows—yes, at moments like this, the TV seemed like a blessing. If her kids weren't riveted by reruns of *Sesame Street* (it was all about letters and numbers, how bad could it be?), they'd still be at each other's throats.

Thank goodness it was June, and the end of the year. Things with Felix were getting intolerable. Kindergarten hadn't been like this, but back then, Felix had a wonderful teacher who understood his need for physical activity. Suddenly, in first grade, he'd had to sit at a desk. Felix had survived, though he'd developed a wicked nail-biting habit. The therapist she and Ron consulted advised them to let it go. It took all of Priscilla's restraint to keep quiet when Felix gnawed on his already-worn fingertips. Something had to change. It had to.

Priscilla poured a generous amount of oil into the skillet and turned on the stove to warm it. These chicken strips were Felix's favorite. She planned to make them again next week, to entice him to come to the homeschooling group's potluck without a fuss. Fortunately Gabby would come along with a smile, no matter what.

Footfalls sounded on the front steps and the door creaked open. "Daaaaddddyy," yelled Felix, leaping up to meet his father. Gabby wasn't far behind. Priscilla heard Ron greeting the kids, and the sounds of kisses being exchanged. She smiled.

"Hey, babe," he said, coming into the kitchen with a kid on each hip.

"Hi," she said, turning her face toward him for a quick kiss. She'd just dipped the first chicken strip into the egg and dredged it in the almond meal, so a hug was out of the question.

"Daddy, come see my dragon." Felix had spent more than an hour after school in his room, with his Playmobil castle, trying to keep Gabby away and lay out one of his elaborate medieval scenarios at the same time. Their intolerable bickering finally drove Priscilla to resort to *Sesame Street*.

Cookie Monster's deep, silly voice blared from the living room. Ron turned toward the sound. "Why is the TV on?"

"They wanted to watch a show," Priscilla said, dropping a piece of chicken into the sizzling oil.

"I thought we talked about that," said Ron. Priscilla knew he didn't like her using the TV when she got frazzled or needed to do something undisturbed, but sometimes she just had to.

"It's just *Sesame Street*," said Priscilla. "Letters. I thought it might help." Felix's teacher had set him up with a resource special-ist because of his difficulty with reading.

"Help with what?" said Ron. "You?"

"Daddy," Felix was pulling on Ron's suit jacket. "Come see."

Ron left with the kids, his question unanswered. Sometimes it felt to Priscilla like Ron didn't want to hear about her problems, he just wanted her to solve them and be perfect.

She took another deep breath, trying to will away her annoy-ance. Ron had no clue what it was like. His idea was to put Felix into an after-school program, where there'd be educational pro-gramming and social interaction. Then she could go back to work in the fall, when Gabby started kindergarten, just like they'd planned.

Priscilla missed her career as a nurse, but Felix, as difficult a time as she was having with him, pulled her. He hated school, and she felt each day he spent there snuffed out his enthusiasm a little bit more. The times when things did come together, when she and the kids fell into a synergy, when she was reading to them, or they were making cookies, taking a walk in the woods, or just talking, felt precious to her.

It was Felix's unhappiness that made her look into home-schooling in the first place, but the moments of familial bliss, and the promise of more, were what made her want to do it. She'd done some Internet research, found a support group, and gone to a meeting. Home Learning Together, it was called, HoLT for short, because of some guy named John Holt. Priscilla had already devoured one of his books, *How Children Fail.* She was working her courage up to read *Teach Your Own.* Although she was already thinking seriously about homeschooling, reading an actual book on the subject felt perilously close to commitment.

Perilous, because Ron was against it, and there was enough ten-sion in their marriage already. Still, when the parents she'd met at HoLT talked about their lives, excitement and longing rose in her.

Those parents made her feel as if she could do it. She felt simpatico with them in a way she never felt when the moms from her preschool group talked about kindergarten readiness. The other parents at the support meeting seemed familiar with the kind of pushback she was getting from Ron. "That's very common," said Carmen. The meeting had been at her house, and her three children had been home. Priscilla had seen them wandering in and out of the living room to show Carmen a picture they'd painted, or leisurely heading to the kitchen to get snacks. Priscilla was impressed when Elizabeth, the oldest, who looked like she was almost a teenager, met her eyes and smiled in greeting.

"My wife was like that at first," said Sam. "She said no way, absolutely not." Sam laughed, and the sound made Priscilla feel at ease. "Look, I said. I'm the one staying home with the kids, and I want to try it."

The story had made Priscilla feel so hopeful, but her hopes were dashed quickly when she got home. Ron was furious she'd even gone to the meeting. He'd been at a work meeting of his own, and she'd been afraid to tell him in person she was going. Instead, she did it in a note on the kitchen table and left the kids with a babysitter.

"What the hell, Priscilla?" Ron had said when she walked in the door. She launched into telling him about the meeting, but he cut her off right away. "I don't want to hear about it. Our kids are not going to be some weird, socially inept, spelling bee contestants."

"But you don't know anything about it," Priscilla countered.

"I know enough," he said.

She remembered the advice Pina had given her. "Ron," Priscilla said. "Would you at least read about it?" He didn't answer. "There's a potluck in a couple weeks at Teresa's house. I want us to go."

Ron looked at her. "Me and you?"

"And the kids."

He didn't answer, just went into the bathroom to brush his teeth. Priscilla took that as a good sign. The next day, they'd spent

22

their whole therapy session on it, and Ron grudgingly agreed to go to the potluck. In the days that followed, Priscilla printed out some articles from the Internet and left them on his night table, along with the *HoLT Directory of Families* that Teresa had emailed her. He didn't admit to reading any of it, but Priscilla thought the pile had at least been touched.

"Mommy, mommy." Gabby came running in to show her a picture.

"That's beautiful, sweetie," said Priscilla, transferring a few more chicken strips to a paper towel-covered plate.

"But you're not looking," said Gabby.

Priscilla turned off the skillet, wiped her hands on a towel, and squatted to be at eye level with Gabby. "OK," she said. "Now I'm looking."

"This is our house," said Gabby, pointing to a blue blob in the middle of the page. "And here's me and you and Daddy."

"Where's Felix?" asked Priscilla.

"He's shut up in his room." Gabby frowned when she said it.

Priscilla's impulse was to tell her she should have put her brother in the picture, or else rave about what a wonderful artist her daughter was, but she decided to try something else. "I like the way you made us all different colors," she said. "It makes each of us unique." Gabby's smile practically glowed. "I have to finish cooking now," said Priscilla.

"So we can eat dinner," said Gabby.

"Yes," said Ron, coming back into the kitchen with Felix. He seemed in a better mood, and Priscilla felt relieved. "Can I help with anything?" he asked.

"Grab a plate so I can arrange the chicken on it," said Priscilla.

"I want to help," said Felix, in a whinier tone than Priscilla would have liked.

"OK," she said. "Why don't you get the honey mustard sauce out of the refrigerator, and a little bowl to put it in."

Felix sprang into action. The second he opened the fridge Gabby turned to her and said, "I want to help, too."

"Here," said Ron, lifting Gabby up. "Help me put the chicken on this platter."

"Goody," said Gabby, looking at the plate. "You know what? We can make a picture with them!"

Ron laughed and they set to work. Felix came over with the plastic container of sauce and a bowl. "I think that one might be too big," said Priscilla. "Can you find another?"

Felix turned to Ron. "Help me find one, Dad?"

Ron opened a cabinet, and waited until Felix pointed to a small red bowl. "That one."

"Great," said Priscilla. "Now let's put the sauce in it."

When they were done, Priscilla set the platter on the table. It wouldn't make it into *Gourmet* magazine, but it looked pretty good.

She turned to Ron. "That was fun, wasn't it?"

He smiled and kissed her quickly. "Let's eat, kids," he said.

"NEXT week we find out our teachers for next year," said Felix, his mouth full of chicken.

Priscilla started to speak but Ron put his hand on hers. "That's great, buddy," said Ron. "I hope you get your first choice."

Felix looked blankly at his father.

"Actually," said Priscilla, screwing up her courage. "Who knows what you'll be doing next year."

Ron glared at her.

"Huh?" said Felix, looking more confused than ever.

Gabby said, "Mommy, why is Daddy giving you stink eye?"

Ron laughed in spite of himself and Priscilla breathed a sigh of relief. "What Mommy means," said Ron, "is that we're going to a homeschooling potluck next week."

"What's that?" asked Felix.

"Some kids don't go to school," said Priscilla. "They learn at home."

"You mean I don't have to go to school?" Felix sounded astonished.

"Don't get any ideas, kid," said Ron. "It's a big long shot."

"What's this potluck?" Felix sounded suspicious.

"It's like a party," said Priscilla. "Other kids will be there."

"Nobody I know, though, right?"

"You'll get to know them," said Priscilla. Felix frowned. "We're going to bring chicken strips, and you can help make them."

He looked slightly more amenable, but not much. Priscilla knew that come potluck night, they might have to carry him out of the house kicking and screaming.

"Well," said Gabby, straightening herself up in her chair and lifting her chin high. "I'm sure it will be a fabulous time."

Ron laughed so hard he cried, which made Felix laugh, which made Gabby laugh, too. Priscilla smiled, and hoped Gabby would turn out to be right.

CHAPTER 3

Zoe

Wednesday, June 12

DEAR Diary,

Today the park was good. I touched the Frisbee at least three times, and I even intercepted a pass. Yeah, I lost it right away, but who cares, besides Elizabeth. Otto wouldn't, I'm sure of that.

Did I mention that I love Otto? He's the ONLY one who gets his submissions in for *Acorn* on time. And he's never called me a Luddite, although I wouldn't care if he did. I like old-fashioned things, and there's nothing wrong with that.

If Elizabeth and Isaac and the rest of the slackers don't get their stuff to me by the end of the week, I'm going to have to delay publication, which will really piss me off. What's people's problem, anyway? If you say you're going to do something, you should do it. It's fun being editor of your own literary magazine, but it ain't easy. Thank goodness Otto is going to help me with the layout, and Dad is going to print copies at his office.

Speaking of Dad, he's been working too hard. I wonder if something is going on with him and Mom. She seems kind of distant, like when I ask her questions she doesn't even hear them half the time, and I'm pretty sure they were arguing in their bedroom last night. I tried to listen but it just sounded like mumbling. I don't know why I care so much. It's not like they never argue, mostly about Jacob. I don't know why, exactly, but I get the feeling something's up with Mom. Yesterday she was talking to Teresa on the phone and I heard her say she wasn't sure we'd be able to go to the potluck. Hello??? We ALWAYS go to the pot-lucks, and this month's is at Teresa's house, and that means I get to hang out with Otto and maybe get him to show me his ideas for the layout.

Then I heard Mom tell Teresa everything was OK, she was just tired. Well, she's always tired, that's nothing new. When she hung up I told her I really wanted to go to the potluck and she said we would. I asked her why she told Teresa we might not and she just said she didn't know.

Then Jacob came barreling inside with his basketball and Mom yelled at him to take it outside, then before he could do it, she said like an afterthought, "Did you do your math today?"

He was gone before he could answer. Anybody could have told her the answer, though. DUH, NO. Jacob hates schoolwork but that doesn't stop Mom from trying to get him to do it all the time. Sometimes I hear her telling Dad that maybe they should send Jacob back to school, but Dad doesn't want to.

He's right, of course. Jacob's been a new kid since he started homeschooling. Happy, and not so much of a pain. Also, if they'd never caved in and started homeschooling him out of desperation, I never would have figured out that

I should do it, too, and it's definitely improved my life A LOT.

So back to what happened earlier, which is SUPER EXCITING. Before Mom could get into it with Jacob, I went back in my room to write some poems and read the neuroscience textbook that Elizabeth's dad didn't need anymore. I found out the coolest things ever about how the brain interacts with all these other body systems. Like where does the brain end and the body begin??? Dad is going to help me figure out other ways I can learn about brains. He said maybe Elizabeth's dad would let us tour his lab.

I know I said the park was good, and it was, mostly, but something weird happened. I was sitting with Otto, and we were talking, but he kept looking over at Elizabeth and Isaac and Cora. After a couple of minutes of Otto getting distracted it started making me mad, but I didn't say anything. Then Elizabeth started coming over to us and Otto started acting weird, squirming and fidgeting and stuff like that.

She only came over to ask if she could get a ride to book group, and I might have answered her except it was obvious she wasn't talking to me. Otto wasn't answering, either—he was rummaging through his backpack. He pulled out an iPod and handed it to Elizabeth. She didn't take it right away, just got this obnoxious look on her face, like, why are you giving this to me and why aren't you answering my question.

Even though she was trying to be cool, I could see she was excited, and why not? Even a Luddite like me would be into an iPod. Then Otto said he didn't need it anymore, and it had Kendrick Lamar's new album on it, and Elizabeth's eyes lit right up. At book group last week she was talking all about how she wanted the album but her mom wouldn't buy it for her and really didn't want her listening to it. I was pretty sure she was full of it, and she hadn't even talked to Carmen about it, but Carmen does like her kids to be coolish nerdly types that aren't into popular culture.

I found myself getting really upset, like, way more upset than I needed to. Why didn't Otto ask ME if I wanted the iPod??? Even though Elizabeth hadn't asked me, I told her we'd give her a ride to book group, just so she would leave. She shrugged and thank goodness started to go, but then Otto said, "No, that's OK, we'll give you a ride."

Elizabeth threw up her hands and smiled, like, oh, great, fight over me, everyone else does. I just muttered OK and then she left, and I asked Otto why he gave Elizabeth that iPod. He got kind of shy and muttered that it was because she wanted it, and then it hit me. OTTO LIKES ELIZABETH.

Diary, you know that even though I complain about Elizabeth and her princess-ness, she is my friend, but thinking that Otto might like her makes me SO MAD. I have to ask myself why. Do I like Otto? I mean, he is my favorite friend ever, but do I like him as more than that?

I just don't know, and I really don't want to think about it. I want to think about the brain and writing poems and finishing *Acorn*, and thank goodness that stuff is always there for me, unlike friends, who can be so damn fickle.

Oh, Mom is calling me. She probably wants me to help her with dinner so she can work on spelling with Jacob. Such a waste of time. The more she makes him do it, the more he fights. He wrote an article about basketball for *Acorn*, and even though I don't think I'll use it, it was pretty obvious he can spell just fine if he wants to. If Mom asked my advice, I'd tell her to quit worrying about Jacob so much. But she doesn't ask me, which I suppose makes sense.

There she is again, and yup, she wants me to bake something for Presentation Night tomorrow. Apparently, that's the only way we're going to go, so obviously I will do it. I'm thinking those fancy Pistachio Lemon Squares. Otto ate about six of them when I made them for book group. Off I go to chop pistachios.

Yours in Poetry,

Zoe

DEAR Diary,

Two entries in one day. Wow, you'd think I don't have a life or something. But I DO have a life, I SO DO, and that's exactly WHY I need two entries.

So I finished baking the lemon bars—best batch ever if I do say so myself—and while I was doing it I was thinking about book group today, which I hadn't told you about before.

I guess I was already feeling annoyed with Elizabeth because of the park incident—well, not really an incident exactly but you know what I mean. So when we got to book group and she went straight for the good chair, it really annoyed me. I mean, why should it, everyone wants to sit in that chair and everyone tries for it, especially the boys.

It seemed to piss off Cora, too, at least that's how it appeared judging by the dirty look she gave Elizabeth, but of course Elizabeth just gave her a smile which made me fume even more. Cora is a really nice kid and actually a way better friend to me than Elizabeth, so why do I gravitate to Elizabeth???

I went to get more chairs, like I always do, and tried to focus on why I was there, to talk about *Frankenstein*, a book which I was totally loving. So we get started and Elizabeth starts talking about how cool Victor Frankenstein is, which isn't true at all, and I'm thinking to myself, what does it say about her that she LIKES the biggest jerk in the book? I mean, I know he's complicated and all that, and I know I finished and Elizabeth probably didn't, but LIKING him is just wrong.

At one point Elizabeth talked about how smart he was and Otto actually agreed with her. Geez, the day was going from bad to worse. During snack he went over to her chair to talk. So there's Elizabeth and Otto chatting away, and Diary, I JUST COULDN'T STAND IT. He's disappointing me, and I hate it when people I like disappoint me. I mean, I've always accepted Elizabeth and her stupid princess tendencies—or at least until now—but I never thought Otto would get taken in. Then again, I guess I'm taken in by her.

I really hope Otto doesn't like Elizabeth. I really hope Presentation Night isn't too weird. At least Cora and I are becoming good friends. She's not as flashy as Elizabeth, but she's really smart and I feel like I can trust her.

Your loyal partner in trying to figure it all out,
Zoe

Presentation Night

Home Learning Together
Thursday, June 13

Mineral display.. Rock Swanson

Fairy world .... Emma Wells

Yellow Submarine.. Tyler & Jasper
Falk-Parsons

Interactive Multiplication Table .... Joy Swanson

Deinonychus antirrhopus model .... Tarek Abbas

Mary's monologue from
The Secret Garden... Anne Wells

Karate kata .... Jacob Bennison-
Wright

Pottery.. Willy Stiles

Rainbow layer cake .... Vera Hornick

Intermission

Modern dance improvisation to Mendelssohn's
Midsummer Night's Dream op. 61 .... Aria Morelli

Cursive book report: *Matilda*.. Sky Swanson

Für Elise by Beethoven and one of
Isaac's own piano compositions................................... Isaac Stiles

Liebesleid by Kreisler on violin.................................... Dominic Morelli

Danse Macabre
by Camille Saint-Saëns on flute .... Elizabeth Wells

Original Poetry .... Zoe Bennison-
Wright

Both Sides Now by Joni Mitchell
sung a cappella.. Cora Lee

Musical Light Show with Raspberry Pi .... Otto Hornick

Yoga dance.. Jewel Swanson

CHAPTER 4

Anthony

Thursday, June 13

Anthony Morelli @Anteater 2h
#homeschoolers are at it again #PresentationNight
#seriousbragging

Anthony Morelli @Anteater 2h
Rock shows us his rocks! #cantmakethisstuffup

Anthony Morelli @Anteater 2h
Emma's cute, I don't know about her fairy house
#sticksandstones

Anthony Morelli @Anteater 2h
Tyler & Jasper kill it! #yellowsubmarine

Anthony Morelli @Anteater 2h
Multiplication tables????? OH JOY #oppositeofjoy #whats6x9
#whats7x4 #whats3x6

Anthony Morelli @Anteater 1h
go Tarek #LegoDinosTakeOverTheWorld

Anthony Morelli @Anteater 1h
Brat plays brat #artimitateslife #notsosecretgarden

Anthony Morelli @Anteater 1h
remind me never to meet this kid in a dark alley. mean karate kicks
my man Jacob! #homeschoolersrule

Anthony Morelli @Anteater 1h
Not a bad bowl, not bad at all #creativehomeschoolers

Anthony Morelli @Anteater 1h
When can we eat it?? #thankyouvera #bestpresentationyet

Anthony Morelli @Anteater 1h
break time! finally the cake is cut I LOVE YOU VERA
#bestbakerever

Anthony Morelli @Anteater 1h
my sister thinks she's isadora duncan #ariathedancefreak

Anthony Morelli @Anteater 1h
Book report?? IN CURSIVE??? #poorsky
#shewantstoBEmatilda

Anthony Morelli @Anteater 58m
fur elise followed by an original work?? #stickwithbeethoven

Anthony Morelli @Anteater 48m
Lucy sings #twinkletwinkle but she ain't supposed to #nomanners

Anthony Morelli @Anteater 46m
WHOA GROSS brownies on the piano #tuckontheloose

Anthony Morelli @Anteater 36m
I have to listen to this all day at home #Dominicstrikesagain
#fiddlefanatic

Anthony Morelli @Anteater 26m
Flute is hard #gladimnotadog

Anthony Morelli @Anteater 22m
mizz zoe tells it #poetryinmotion

Anthony Morelli @Anteater 21m
I like you, Zoe, but one poem was enough #nuffsaid

Anthony Morelli @Anteater 17m
what else to say but this, I didn't know cora could sing
#seriouspipes

Anthony Morelli @Anteater 13m
YYYYAAAAAAASSSSS Otto!!! 👌 🎵 ☺ #worldinlights
#raspberrypirules

Anthony Morelli @Anteater 55s
somebody tell jewel that yoga is for exercising not performing
#parentscanbesoembarrassing

CHAPTER 5

Potluck Invitation

Friday, June 14

From: TereesieE
Sent: 6/14/2015 1:38 PM
To: HoLT
Subject: [HoLT] June potluck!

Hi Everyone,

I hope everyone's year has been as great as ours! It was
wonderful to see so many talents and accomplishments on
display at Presentation Night. On the heels of that, it's time
for another annual celebration—the HoLT June Potluck!
Come on over to my house at 67 Washburn Place for good
food and fun, 6-9 p.m. on June 20. We have plenty of room
and space in the backyard for kids to play. RSVPs
appreciated but not required. Most of you know our
charming pug Romeo, but for those who don't, FYI we have
a dog. Hope to see you all here!

Cheers,
Teresa

From: PinaAndCompany
Sent: 6/14/2015 2:01 PM
To: HoLT
Subject: RE: [HoLT] June potluck!

Yay, our favorite event of the year! We'll be there with Mac
& Cheese. Can't wait!

Pina

From: ElizabethIsHere
Sent: 6/14/2015 4:30 PM
To: HoLT
Subject: RE: [HoLT] June potluck!

Mom will make empanadas. I'm making chocolate peanut
butter pie.

Elizabeth

From: AliceBillKids
Sent: 6/14/2015 6:47 PM
To: HoLT
Subject: RE: [HoLT] June potluck!

We'll all be there and we'll bring lasagne!

Alice

From: ZoeGirl
Sent: 6/14/2015 7:45 PM
To: HoLT
Subject: RE: [HoLT] June potluck!

Not sure how many from my family will be there, but I will make pistachio lemon squares (AGAIN!).

Thanks!!!
Zoe

From: SamontheHorn
Sent: 6/14/2015 8:11 PM
To: HoLT
Subject: RE: [HoLT] June potluck!

Hi Everyone,

Thanks for hosting, Teresa! All four of us will be there with a vegan salad. Good idea to remember labeling dishes with ingredients for those with special dietary needs. I know a family that came to the last support meeting is coming, and they're gluten-free. Looking forward!

Sam

From: BreatheDeep
Sent: 6/14/2015 8:45 PM
To: HoLT
Subject: RE: [HoLT] June potluck!

Oh, my mouth is watering! We're planning to be there with something vegetarian. Thank you, Teresa!

Jewel

From: Nasim&Sarah&Tarek
Sent: 6/14/2015 9:31 PM
To: HoLT
Subject: RE: [HoLT] June potluck!

We'll certainly be there, not sure yet with what.

Sarah

CHAPTER 6

Carmen

Friday, June 14

DEAR V.,

I miss you. I miss experiencing the mundane with you. While I do appreciate the opportunity to actually hold a pen and manipulate it with my hand, I don't know how long I can keep it up. Hopefully long enough to catch you up on EVERYTHING.

The girls are good. Elizabeth as usual seems to be master of all she surveys. I'm so glad she's avoided the loss of self that's so common in pubescent girls. She's got enough self for the two of us! Maybe for the whole family! Anyway, she's still doing Pina's book group, playing Frisbee on Wednesdays, and she's planning to sign up for a class at the community college in the fall. She is gung-ho and wanted to do two but I encouraged her to start with one and see how it goes. I don't want her to be overwhelmed. If it's something she likes, there's plenty of opportunity.

In general she marches to her own drummer, but I wonder if part of the attraction with the college classes is that some of the older kids are taking them, and she wants to spread her wings and join them. I know it's inevitable, but she's still only 12! Well, we'll see how it goes. She's going to do Intro to Spanish, so she already has some familiarity with it from me speaking Spanish at home (not enough!) y con sus abuelos.

Anyway, lately I've been feeling guilty that so much of my time and attention is focused on Elizabeth and the little girls get neglected. Especially Anne. She just goes along and makes so few demands, and I guess I take advantage of her easy going-ness. It's like she's in Elizabeth's shadow. Extending the metaphor, Lizzie's the sun and we're all revolving around her. Except Henry, who's some kind of satellite in his own orbit. Lizzie's energy and her millions of ideas make it hard not to be drawn along.

I've been organizing regular trips to the Museum of Science, the last one a week or so ago. Overall it was fine, but I just feel like I'm always doing for others, and I'm worn out. Henry's been away for work a lot—I know, nothing new—but it's hard parenting alone for so much of the time. Plus I'm happy when he's home, but it throws off the rhythm around here quite a bit. Sort of between a rock and a hard place I guess. But I digress. At the Museum, Nasim was nice enough to take the little girls so I could go to the Maya exhibit with Elizabeth. But then at lunch I felt like I couldn't sit with everyone else because they were buying junk food from the cafeteria and I didn't want my girls to get ideas. So I ended up sitting with Alice.

I know I know! Alice is lovely in her dreamlike way, but you wouldn't believe what happened at Presentation Night. Or maybe you would believe. Of course Lucy wanted to perform, I don't know why Alice didn't just sign her up in the first place, but she didn't. But not a big deal—I let her go up after Isaac played piano. It was very sweet. But THEN, Tuck appears on the stage, hands and face covered with gooey brownie and proceeds to smear it all over the piano. I'm hoping to see Alice rising from her chair to intervene, but no! There she sits wearing her beatific smile, gazing at Tuck, and obliviously nursing Silas. Ay! Luckily Kevin, their piano teacher, was pretty fast on the uptake and swooped in for Tuck before too much damage was done. I don't know how people expect us to continue to be able to use the space if we don't respect it.

It's the abuse of rental space, but also the not showing up to field trips. Both affect me personally, and also I worry about the perception of homeschoolers when I organize an event and then half (or sometimes even more!) of the people who signed up don't show. Was it always this way? I feel that it's gotten worse, and I'm not sure why. Maybe people overschedule and don't realize they are inconveniencing a real live person. Not to mention it just makes me feel like a loser—why am I putting myself out there if no one appreciates it? Honestly sometimes I just call around to a few people I know the girls want to hang out with and arrange to meet privately. And I'm not going to feel guilty about it!

I better think of something else to write about besides poor little me. So, on the bright side it was really great at Presentation Night to see all the different things the kids have been up to this year. I'll send you the program. Lizzie tells me that Anthony "live tweeted" the whole event. I don't expect you to have a clue what that means—ask one of your kids.

Pina is an angel to do book group week after week. The kids really have a kind of home base, something they feel a part of. And then of course there're the books. By now I

45

think Lizzie's read more than I have. Pina certainly picks some novels I wouldn't have thought of. Speaking of Pina, looks like she's put on some weight. Every time I see her around food she goes right for the sweets. Not sure what that's about.

Anyway, one great thing about book group is that I can count on two hours every week to spend time with the little girls. Anne's been hinting that she'd like to have more acting opportunities. She was in the local children's theater production of *The Secret Garden*. Of course she wanted to be Mary, but she got cast in a bit part. She brilliantly thought to do one of Mary's monologues for Presentation Night, so got to work on the character after all.

As you know, I always leave the arts and crafts supplies accessible. No V., not just for me—for the girls! In general Emma is a fan, but lately, as the weather's warmed up, she's gotten into the idea of fairy worlds. Conveniently, a lot of that takes place in the yard, with stuff she finds. She creates little houses and landscapes with bits of moss and bark, pebbles, leaves, sticks. Whatever she finds! And her eye is always out for the odd stone or seed pod wherever we go. She creates storylines to go along with all of her creations. When I'm at the kitchen sink, I can hear her running narration from the open window. For Presentation Night she wanted to somehow show off these creations, so we had the idea for her to make one in a flower pot. If her interest holds out, I'll get some books about terrariums from the library for her.

Ack! That reminds me—thank goodness Emma's fairy house didn't get destroyed at Presentation Night like Tarek's Lego creation did! It's a "mystery"—the tail end of his dinosaur was broken off, and we found Lego pieces far and wide when we swept up at the end of the night. No one claimed responsibility, but you know who I think did it, right? Tarek wasn't happy about it, but Nasim downplayed the incident. With everyone presumed innocent until proven guilty, we may never know what really happened.

Remember that single mom, Ellen, I told you about? Lizzie's getting to be good friends with her daughter Cora. I talked to Ellen some at the geography fair a couple weeks ago. Terrifies me. I feel like a single mom since I fly solo so much of the time, but Henry does provide a paycheck. I don't know what I would do if something happened to him, or, to us. I haven't worked since Lizzie was born, and while I still paint, I haven't done much to keep up any professional contacts. Ellen is an editor, so she works from home. How would I support us? Home daycare? Or maybe the girls would have to go to school, and I'd take anything I could get. I try not to think about it, but then I think maybe that's stupid, and I should try to cultivate something. There must be some way to parlay all the stuff I do as a home-school mom into getting paid.

Well, V. I guess I'm showing my hand here. I feel like Henry and I live separate lives. I'm so caught up in the girls, and even when Henry's home, he is preoccupied with work demands. I feel like I can't justify asking him to pay more attention to me. As he readily points out, he has a job! He's paying the bills! Is he just stressed out, or not interested? I'm afraid to ask. Maybe it's time for me to make some money. Maybe that would level the field a little, and also make me a little less anxious about what might happen.

I'm hoping we can get out to see you soon on your idyllic farm, surrounded by baby goats and chicks. Will you ever come to visit us again? I need to hear all about your kids (the human ones), and how things are going with meeting new friends out in the boonies.

Love and kisses,

Carmen

CARMEN set down her pen and sighed. Writing was cathartic, but she felt a bit like her letters to V. were entering a void. She hadn't heard back from her in months. V.'s visit shortly after she first moved seemed ages ago. She'd come back to town once, unannounced, to tie up loose ends, and managed to make it to the park so the kids could run off some steam, but Carmen hadn't gotten any alone time with her. V. had insisted she couldn't even stop by Carmen's for a quick lunch before her drive back to the farm, citing traffic concerns.

Carmen reached for her cup of chai and found it had gone cold. Yuck. And it was already 5:45. She'd have to think of something to put on the table for dinner.

She pushed back from the desk, her chair scraping against the wood floor, leaving another scratch. No question, after all these years of homeschooling, her house had that "lived in" look. A house full of projects, including her own, precluded a picture perfect home. Still, she prided herself on maintaining a level of taste and comfort in the décor that she felt expressed who she was. She exited the relative quiet of her bedroom and descended the stairs to the doorway of the brightly lit kitchen.

"Whoa! What's going on in here?"

"Mother dear, I am testing a new recipe I plan to bring to the potluck," Elizabeth chirped. She looked up from the pie dish into which she'd been pressing what looked like a chocolate cookie crumb crust. The little girls sat at the counter in rapt attention. Emma was licking a spatula and Anne was nibbling from an open bag of chocolate chips. The kitchen counter was strewn with bowls and spatulas, and the electric mixer was set up, some goo dripping from its beaters.

"What is that smell?" Carmen asked, crinkling her nose.

"Oh I think the mixer's engine may be burning out."

"Great. You may have to revert to the good ol' egg beater method. I came in thinking it was about dinner time. But I'm out of interesting ideas."

She drew up a stool and pinched a piece of the crust for a nibble. Elizabeth's hand whipped out to swat her away. "Mom! I'm not done."

"OK, sorry. Tastes good. How about soup and sandwiches for dinner?"

"Fine by me. As long as we can have this pie for dessert." said Elizabeth.

"Anne, will you look and see what soup we have on hand?"

Anne hopped down and opened the Lazy Susan. She twirled it around and then grabbed it to slow it down some. "Looks like tomato."

"Grilled cheese and tomato soup it is then. Let's get it started."

After dinner, the four of them went out on the porch for dessert. Carmen sat on the stairs. The pie had turned out tasty but soupy—it needed to chill longer. She ate it slowly, and tried to spot fireflies as they blinked in the garden. The summer ahead stretched out in front of her. She had allowed each of her daughters to choose one summer activity. Elizabeth had chosen learning to sail at the program in the harbor. Some of the older kids were planning on it, and—it should come as no surprise—Elizabeth wanted to hang out with them, but it seemed to Carmen that she had grown up overnight. Once the weeklong program finished, Elizabeth would have access to open sailing throughout the summer. She also planned to promote her pet sitting business in an attempt to make some spending money. While Carmen admired her ambition, she had an inkling that she herself would end up with a bunch of the work, once the charm had worn off for Elizabeth.

Anne had her heart set on the local children's theater production. That would extend across weeks, but it didn't get really intense until tech week. Of course part of the deal was that parents were required to volunteer. Carmen hoped there would be help needed with costuming, as sewing was something she was good at and enjoyed. Plus she could do it on her own time, late at night when things had quieted down in the house.

Emma had opted for a half day program at a wildlife center and farm, where she'd get to learn about taking care of the animals and other farm work. It sounded like a lot of fun, except for the part about getting up at the crack of dawn to get her there on time, and then making a return commute to pick her up mid-afternoon.

At least homeschool activities tended to slow down over the summer. It was a different pace, but also a lonelier time. With families taking vacation and kids signed up for summer activities, attendance at park day was irregular. Maybe sometime over the summer, she'd be able to make a date to hang out with Teresa and Pina and a couple other women. Some adult time would be welcome.

Hopefully Henry would be able to take some time off at the end of the summer. Some of her best memories were the ones of camping as a family. Well, she'd go with him or without him.

Licking her spoon, she rose and went to put her dish in the sink. The girls followed with theirs. Carmen turned the water on to rinse them and swung around, hoping to snag one of them to help with washing up, but they'd all hightailed it out of there. She dried her hands on the dishtowel and picked up the phone to dial Henry's cell. The call went to voicemail and she hung up without leaving a message.

"Hey girls—it's still light out. Who wants to walk down to the pond and see if we catch the sunset?"

Anne and Emma abandoned their knitting and joined her. Elizabeth was engrossed in something on the computer.

"Lizzie, do you want to join us?

"No thanks mom. I'm just in the middle of a conversation."

Carmen stood at the door for a moment, a hand on each of her little girls' heads, looking at the back of her eldest's. A year ago Lizzie would have been the instigator, but her priorities were changing. Carmen wasn't keen on a lot of computer time, but she was glad that it enabled Lizzie to connect with her friends.

"OK. We'll be back in a few minutes then."

Carmen and the little girls bustled out the door and walked the couple blocks to the pond. "Mommy?" Emma swung around in front of her and stopped. "I want to bring something to the potluck too."

Anne joined in with "Good idea!"

"You mean it's not enough to just bring Lizzie's pie?"

There was a chorus of "NOOOO."

Carmen had been hoping that Lizzie's efforts would get her out of making something, but clearly the girls had other plans. "Do you have something in mind?"

Emma tilted her head and looked up at her mom. "Empanadas."

"Lizzie suggested it," said Anne.

Carmen could hardly say no to that comfort food. But talk about a production. Oh well, of course she'd agree.

Having checked in on the Mallard family, thrown a few stones into the pond, and contemplated the concentric circles on the surface of the water, they turned back and headed home. Carmen could see through the window that Lizzie was still on the computer. She shooed Emma and Anne upstairs to get ready for bed. The phone rang. Maybe it was Henry calling her back.

Carmen shrugged off her sweater and grabbed the kitchen extension. "Hello?"

"Hi Carmen. It's Teresa."

"Oh hi. What's up?"

"Just checking in, saying hi. You're bringing empanadas to the potluck, right?"

"Wait a minute—I just found that out myself. How did *you* know?"

"Lizzie RSVPed on the HoLT list."

"I should have known. I guess for this crowd I'll have to throw together some vegetarian ones along with my traditional meat."

"Yeah. I guess I'm just going to make a pot of chili. Is Henry going to come?"

"I'm not sure. If he's home from his trip he will. I tried to call him tonight but I didn't get through."

"That's frustrating."

"Yes. I can't really count on him. I guess I've gotten used to it, but then sometimes I wonder—" She was interrupted by Emma, who had changed into her nightgown but was now standing in front of Carmen demanding a cup of tea and a bedtime story. Carmen's hand holding the phone started to sink.

"You were saying?" Teresa's voice trailed from the ear piece.

"Mom! Emma had turned up the volume. "It's bedtime. You said!"

"Teresa, I'm sorry—the girls need me. I've got to go do bed-time."

"You sure they can't give you a couple minutes to chat?"

Carmen looked down into her daughter's set face, and told Teresa no, she had to go. She hung up the phone and set the kettle to boil. She grabbed four mugs and plopped a Sleepytime teabag into each one. By this time Emma had drifted into the living room and was hanging on the back of Lizzie's chair. Carmen tapped her.

"I'll be up in a couple minutes. Go on, OK?"

"I'll wait for you."

"No. Come on. Go up with Anne. I'll bring the tea in a minute."

When the water was hot, she poured it into the waiting mugs and brought one in to Lizzie.

"I'm heading up to read to your sisters. Do you want to come?"

"Thanks Mom, but I'm going to read the stuff for book group when I finish this math chapter."

"OK then." Carmen locked the front door and headed upstairs. In her room, Emma and Anne were waiting for her. She put the tea down and grabbed her PJs. In the bathroom she peed, brushed her teeth, and got changed. Then she nestled into the middle spot on the king-size bed, bolstered by pillows, and began to read aloud *The Penderwicks*. She got through two chapters before she noticed that Emma had dozed off. Anne begged her to finish the chapter they were in the middle of.

"OK sweetie." She finished the third chapter and drew the ribbon of bookmark between the pages. She reached over the slumbering body of her youngest to put the book on the bedside table and switched off the light. Anne snuggled down, determined to stay in the big bed as well. Carmen looked out at the moon, which shone in brightly through the gauzy white curtains. She reached for her tea and took a sip, hoping it would be true to its name.

CHAPTER 7

Ellen

Tuesday, June 18

"LET'S go, Cora." Ellen raked through her bag for the hundredth time, searching for her tablet. She had a tendency to misplace it, but why today? Today of all days, when she had a meeting with a potential new client, a professor who could provide steady work for at least a little while, something which god knows she needed.

The bag search yielded nothing, so Ellen turned to the living room. A desperate move, but she'd already checked the likely locations. Now it was time to move onto the long shots. As she rummaged through the TV cabinet, her phone buzzed, reminding her that her meeting started in thirty minutes.

To hell with the tablet. She headed for her desk to get her laptop, then remembered it was charging. Oh, to hell with that, too. Paper and pen, just like the old days, which to tell the truth, she really missed.

"Cora!" she yelled, grabbing a notebook and her purse. "Come now or I can't give you a ride. I'm going to be late as it is." That wasn't technically true—at least she hoped it wouldn't be. It all depended on traffic.

"Yeah, Mom," said Cora. Ellen turned to see her daughter walking down the hall, her face buried in an electronic device that just happened to be the tablet Ellen had been trying to unearth.

"Cora!" She yanked the tablet away. "I've been going crazy looking for that."

"Sorry, Mom. I had to look something up for my meeting with Zoe."

"Well, I need it for a meeting with a client. And I don't use the word *need* lightly." She'd put the edge in her voice intentionally, but the look on Cora's face made her soften. It wasn't Cora's fault Ellen couldn't afford to buy her a computer, and they had to share devices. "Next time just ask, OK? Now, come on."

Ellen opened the front door and stepped outside, expecting Cora to be right behind her, but halfway down the front steps she turned to see her daughter still inside, leisurely tying her Converse sneakers. "Honey," said Ellen, not sounding at all sweet. "I need to go. Now."

"I know, Mom," she said. "I'm coming."

Finally they were in Ellen's old Hyundai and on their way. "What are you doing at Zoe's?"

"I already told you, we're working on *Acorn.*"

"What's *Acorn?*"

"I told you, it's the magazine Zoe is editing."

"Oh, right," said Ellen. "I forgot." A magazine was so quaint. Leave it to homeschoolers. "What are you writing for it?"

As Cora answered, Ellen calculated in her head how many more minutes it would take to get to the college, park, and walk to her potential client's office. "Damn," she yelled, stopping for yet another red light and interrupting Cora mid-sentence, which didn't matter much, since Ellen hadn't been listening in the first place.

She turned to Cora, trying to refocus, but Cora wasn't talking anymore, she was staring out the window, twirling her ink black hair around her fingers. Ellen reached for her hand and brushed it away from its nervous activity. "Stop."

Cora looked at Ellen and smiled. "Sorry, Mom." She was the sweetest girl, and Ellen loved her like crazy, but sometimes she wished Cora could be as mature as Zoe, who seemed to handle all kinds of projects with competence and organizational aplomb.

The light turned green and Ellen sped away, feeling a stab of guilt at her impatience, her irritability, and her failure to be present for Cora. It was work that did it. These days, she worked too much and got too little for it, a pair of situations she was way too old to be dealing with, but such is life. Really, she was lucky to be alive. James wasn't, and neither were all the plans that had died in the accident with him. She still missed him so much it hurt, and some days Cora was all that kept her going.

Homeschooling had proven challenging, too, which didn't mean that Ellen regretted the decision, or wanted to stop. Hard as it was on Ellen, it was the best thing that ever happened to Cora. Ellen had hoped to be working less as time went on, but things weren't going that way. Rates were going down, not up, and work was harder to come by. She'd thought about trying to land a steady position, but freelancing was so much better for their lifestyle, as long as she could manage to keep the stress from burying her.

"Here we are," Ellen said as she pulled up in front of Zoe's house. Jacob was in the driveway dribbling a basketball next to a parked minivan. Otto and Teresa emerged from it and headed for the house. Teresa might hang out with Melissa, or take the time to do something for herself. Meanwhile, Ellen had to go to work. She felt a flash of envy, followed immediately by a goddamn hot flash. They had a tendency to be triggered by strong emotions, and Ellen was experiencing quite a lot of those. "Say hi to Melissa and Teresa for me," she said as she leaned over to hug Cora.

"Good luck with the meeting, Mom."

Ellen held Cora to her for a precious second. "Thanks, sweetie pie," she said. "I'll see you at home later."

IT WAS almost six by the time Ellen arrived home. The meeting proved longer than she expected, which turned out to be a good thing. The professor liked her references, didn't balk at the rate she quoted, and hired her on the spot to edit his thirteen hundred plus page tome. The subject, feudalism in the Middle Ages, sounded deadly boring, but the professor turned out to be charming. He wanted to get to work right away, which meant Ellen had spent the better part of the afternoon with him going over details. She'd texted Cora to let her know and gotten no response, which wasn't unusual.

"Honey," she called as she opened the unlocked door. Silence. Ellen tried again. "Cora?"

"Hi, Mom." Her tiny voice sounded from her room at the end of the hall. Ellen kicked off her pumps and walked across the floorboards to Cora's door.

"Hey," she said, opening it a smidge. "Can I come in?"

Cora mumbled something affirmative, and Ellen entered and sat down on the edge of the twin bed. Cora was lying on her stomach, typing on Ellen's laptop. "Did you have a good time at Zoe's?" Cora muttered something that sounded vaguely like a yes without averting her eyes from the screen. "What are you working on?"

"Another story."

"About what?"

"Just a story."

The last story Cora wrote broke Ellen's heart, it was so personal. She wanted to know more about this one, but sensed that asking wouldn't yield an answer. "Is that for Zoe's magazine?" Another mumbled affirmative. "Well," said Ellen, standing. "I can't wait to read it." She looked at the clock by Cora's bed. It was dinner time, and she realized she was famished. "Did you have lunch?" Cora shook her head. Ellen didn't like it when Cora skipped meals. It reminded her of when she was getting bullied in school. She'd become so skinny the doctor was concerned about an eating disorder. "How about I make nachos?" said Ellen.

That got Cora's attention. She looked up from the screen and smiled. "Oh, yeah," she said.

Ellen stroked Cora's shiny hair. "OK, kid," she said. "I'll call you when they're ready."

MAKING nachos was meditative.

First, preheat the broiler. Next, spread the tortilla chips on the cookie sheet, then raid the refrigerator for toppings. Ellen found shredded cheddar jack, salsa, half a can of black beans, and some sour cream. She also grabbed the green olives, which Cora loved, and some frozen corn.

She felt like an artist as she applied the ingredients, jagged red lines of salsa, clumps of beans, smatterings of cut-up olives and kernels of corn. This was fun. The whole day, in fact, once she'd gotten to her appointment, had been fun. It had been a long time since she'd landed a job that would hold her in good stead for several months, which would allow her the breathing space to give Cora more of the attention she needed. It had been even longer since she'd worked with someone as fun as Tom—that was the professor's first name, and he'd insisted she use it.

After the nachos were under the broiler for a few minutes, Ellen put on an oven mitt and transferred the tray of sizzling goodness to the table.

"Cora," she called. "They're ready."

Cora sauntered into the kitchen, sat at the table, and went right for a cheesy one with two olives. "Thanks, Mom," she said. "I'm so hungry."

They ate in silence for a couple of minutes, then Cora said, "What are we bringing to the potluck?"

"What potluck?"

"Duh, Mom," said Cora, getting as close to annoyed as she ever did. "The potluck at Otto's. It's coming right up."

Ellen had forgotten all about the potluck, probably because of her ambivalence about going. There were plenty of people she really liked and would love to see, like Teresa and Russell, Pina and Lou, and especially Sam and Stacy, but sometimes being around all those couples depressed her. At least no one would get on her case about why she hadn't started dating again. If she had time to hang around more, she might be able to get to know Teresa or Pina better, or even Melissa, who was the mother of Cora's best friend, after all. Unfortunately, that was about all Ellen could say for her. From what Ellen could see, Melissa was consumed by trying to figure out what to do with Zoe's younger brother Jacob, which was silly. Jacob was active and impulsive, but he was one of the brightest, not to mention nicest, kids Ellen had ever met.

"Mom?" said Cora. "The potluck?"

"Of course we'll go, honey." It would be good to get out, before her deep dive into the serfs and vassals. She'd just have to stay away from Carmen, who asked way too many questions. Ellen didn't want a repeat or continuation of the conversation that had occurred at the geography fair.

It was beyond mortifying. Ellen had been talking to Sam, but Jasper was demanding Sam's attention. That was when Carmen swooped in like some kind of social vulture. She started with compliments about Cora's exhibit on South Korea. Ellen smiled politely but she had a bad feeling about the direction of Carmen's chatter. "So, is Cora liking homeschooling?" Carmen asked.

That was a harmless question. "She loves it," said Ellen, scanning the room to find a way out of the grilling she suspected was coming. Carmen was nosy, and she liked to talk about the details of other people's lives. Ellen understood that on some level. Once upon a time, before her own life had turned into a topsy-turvy mess, Ellen had been interested in people and their stories, too. With Carmen, though, it seemed to go beyond. Pina and Teresa didn't engage when Carmen got going, but they tolerated her politely. Ellen had no desire to be put in that position, and she certainly didn't want Carmen talking about her personal life, or Cora's. The mere thought of it sent her gut into spasm, and Carmen's next comment only made it worse. "I'm sorry about your husband."

Ellen stared open-mouthed at Carmen. "What?"

"Your husband. The car accident. I'm sorry."

Sam was across the room, kneeling before Jasper, engaging in a serious eye-level talk with him. Ellen thought Sam might be a good friend, so she'd confided about James. Sam was the only one she'd told, but now Carmen knew, too. "How do you know that?" Ellen managed to say over the lump in her throat.

"Lizzie told me," said Carmen, oozing sympathy. Ellen felt angry and confused at the same time. Elizabeth? How could she know? Then she heard her daughter's laughter and looked across the room to see her standing in a circle with Zoe and Otto and Elizabeth. It was Cora. Shy Cora, who barely talked to anyone, had talked about her father to these new friends.

Carmen put her hand on Ellen's shoulder, and Ellen recoiled. "Thank you," she said, and walked away briskly.

When they arrived home she asked Cora about it, and Cora confirmed that she had told both Zoe and Elizabeth. "Do you feel OK about it?" asked Ellen.

"Yes, Mom," she said. "It was a long time ago, and I went to plenty of therapy, remember?" She had, with the school psychologist. Cora paused, then added, "I'm more OK than you think, Mom. And I think I'm more OK with it than you are."

The remark stung, but Ellen couldn't deny it. She'd gone to therapy, grief support groups, yoga classes, and more, trying to accept what had happened. She'd definitely come a long way, but while the ache of missing James, the chronic pain left by her injuries, and the anxiety and panic disorder triggered by the accident had waned, they would never completely go away. "I'm sorry, honey," she said. "I'm doing my best."

Cora hugged her. "I just want you to be happy again," she said.

Happiness was something Ellen wanted, too—didn't everyone?—but after everything that had happened to her, it seemed so abstract and unreachable.

Happy moments seemed like the more achievable goal, and as she sat eating one of her favorite foods with her daughter, she felt grateful to be experiencing one. She munched on an especially good nacho and looked at Cora, who was getting so big, so grown-up.

Happy was what Ellen wanted for Cora, too, and thank goodness Cora finally seemed to have arrived. In the year since they'd started homeschooling, she'd blossomed in ways Ellen could never have imagined. She knew that getting away from the bullying made a huge difference, but it was more than that. The quirky kids she'd befriended, the time to get absorbed in things she cared about—those were more healing than any therapy session she could have attended.

Cora liked to hole up in her room a lot, alone, and Ellen had worried about that before realizing that it was partly responsible for restoring peace and balance to her daughter's spirit. She was, after all, an introvert at heart.

"I want to make chocolate hazelnut tarts for the potluck," said Cora. "Zoe really likes them."

"OK," said Ellen.

"Do we have hazelnuts?" asked Cora, eating the last nacho.

"I don't know, but we can get some." The kitchen window was open a smidge, and Ellen felt a warm breeze glide over her. It was a beautiful evening. She looked at Cora. "Are you busy tonight?"

Cora shook her head. "Not really. I just have to finish my story by Friday."

"Are you up for a movie and froyo?"

Cora smiled. "You know I am."

"All right," said Ellen, rising from her chair. She looked at the empty cookie sheet on the table. Her culinary masterpiece had been completely consumed, only specks of salty chips and shining oily residue left on the metal canvas.

She picked up her bag and her keys and turned to her daughter. "Let's go."

ACORN

Squirrel It Away for a Good Read

Volume 1 Issue 3   **Spring 2015**

Queen of Hearts by Cora Lee

Katrina woke up early on Saturday morning. Normally, it was her day to sleep in, but she was too excited. In three hours, she'd be at the Anime convention, watching videos, maybe going to workshops, and definitely hanging with some cool friends.

The most important thing was that Katrina would be hanging with Lila. She really liked Lila, more than anyone she'd ever known. Normally, she'd just wear her regular jeans and sneakers, but she knew Lila was into cosplay, so she spent a whole week putting together an outfit.

After spending the next two hours trying to concentrate on a book, Katrina decided it was finally time to get dressed. She'd put on red tights and a black leotard when her mother knocked on her door. "Katrina, I made pancakes. You need a good breakfast before going to this thing all day."

"Thanks, Mom. I'll be right down." She didn't really want pancakes but she'd eat some just to make her mother happy. Since her dad died, she spent a lot of time trying to make her mother happy.

Over her head went the tunic she'd decorated herself with sewn-on glittery hearts. She wrapped the black patent leather belt around her waist, and put on her black boots and the heart hat she found at the thrift store.

When she looked in the mirror she practically didn't recognize herself, but maybe that was a good thing. Maybe she could be someone new, at least for a day.

In This Issue

Interview with Grown Unschooler Kevin Washington
by Isaac Stiles

How would you describe your homeschooling experience? Advantages, disadvantages? Either when you were little, and/or looking back as an adult.

Well, I would say the biggest disadvantage then and now is that no one appears to "get it." Even today I don't bring it up until people get to know me, because people will start attributing every "weird" part of my personality to the fact that I homeschooled. This results in most people being shocked when they find out. "But you're so normal!" I know—I wasn't raised by wolves, or chained up in the basement; I just didn't show up to school every day, that's the difference. The biggest advantage is I don't have to convince myself to learn—it's still fun. I feel like a collector, a work in progress and I'm a little better every day.

What are some of your favorite memories?

This question is a lot harder than it should be and I'm trying to figure out why. I liked getting into alternatingly funny and serious debates with my friends in book group (whether *Walden* is the best or worst book of all time), deciding whose name would go first à la Lennon/McCartney in our co-written songs, (I got Lennon, score), and getting together to play Frisbee with all my friends once a week. I guess it's hard to choose because homeschooling wasn't somewhere I went 8-3 (is that when people go to school?) every day. It was just my whole life up until college and maybe even after, so it's hard to pick a favorite memory!

How has homeschooling contributed to where you are today? What are your current interests?

It's probably a bigger part of who I am than I can articulate, but because I don't know how I'd have turned out otherwise, it's hard to know. I will say I think it's got a lot to do with the fact that I have many current interests. I never got a distaste for learning. I still like picking up hobbies and reading about new things. Currently I'm trying to learn web development, the Tabla, and the nature of the physical universe (OK, maybe I just finished *Cosmos*).

Did you ever feel anxious about not keeping up, or comparing yourself to kids who went to school?

I don't think I felt anxious that I wasn't able to keep up, but I did get anxious that kids would hear I'm homeschooled and start to quiz me, which was fairly common. Mostly they wanted to know if I memorized the multiplication tables, which I still haven't. I'm sure most of them have forgotten as well, since their adult analogs in my life calculate tips on their iPhones. That wasn't supposed to sound condescending; maybe I'm slightly bitter about that.

Did you ever want to try school?
I don't think I ever really did. By the time I was old enough to consider high school, I had specific interests and the opportunity to take classes in them if I wanted. Before that all my friends who went to school told me I was "soooo lucky" and that was enough for me. I did take some classes though—to see if I could do it, and to prepare for college, which I did want to experience.

How did you learn something if your parents couldn't teach it to you?
Read a book, google it, take a summer program, or get together with a group in the community to learn it. Those are my real answers but I actually didn't think of it that way at the time. I wasn't checking off subjects on a list of things I didn't know yet. I was learning what I was interested in, to the depth that I could handle, more or less until my interests changed. Not to mention that although my parents couldn't teach me everything, they could certainly point me in the right direction, so it wasn't like I had to figure it all out myself.

How would you describe your social life as a homeschooler?
Pretty "normal," whatever that means. I never wanted more friends than I had. I think I had fun times with the usual amount of teenage drama mixed in. I certainly don't feel like I missed out. Well, I was never bullied, so there's something I missed.

How did you adjust to college and working?
Personally I found it a smooth transition. I think the fact that I'd been learning and working for my own benefit the whole time made it easy to find motivation. As opposed to going to college to pass the classes and get a degree, I wanted to get a set of skills out of the experience. I also put pressure on myself to prove that a homeschooler could do as well as or better than their peers, although I don't think about that much anymore.

My Dog by Lucy Stiles

When I got my dog he belonged to a lady. She was letting people have them for some money. We might have gotten another dog named Pokey but we got the dog we wanted. We named him Max. The lady had long fingernails and when she clicked them our dog came. So that's how we got our dog. Before the names in our family were Mommy, Daddy, Isaac, Willy, Lucy and Tuck. Now there is one more, it is Max. The End.

[Ed. note: Since Lucy wrote this another name has been added to her family. It is Silas.]

Mist Fairies by Emma Wells

The mist fairies gently fall and wash the world. As they return to their cloud home they leave their jewels in the grass so they will shine when the sun rises at dawn.

❖ **P O E T R Y C O R N E R** ❖

Frogs
by Zoe Bennison-Wright

You think they're always green
Then one day on a trip
Or in a dream
Boom
They surprise you
Orange eyes
Blue skin
Yellow stripes
Where did they come from,
These differences?
You want to know,
But it's one of those questions with
No answer

Friends by Anne Wells

We are friends
And friends we shall stay
Land nor sea can separate you
    from me
We are bound by love
Although we go our separate
    ways
We are forever bound by love!

We Appreciate Your Support

Acorn is a quarterly publication. We welcome your submissions of writings or drawings to be considered for publication. We cannot return original material.

CHAPTER 8

Sam

Wednesday, June 19

TYLER, where are your shoes?" Sam tried to keep the frustration out of her voice as she rummaged through the ridiculously over-stuffed box next to the front door. Most of the pumps, sandals, and flats were Stacy's, but Jasper's tattered *Guardians of the Galaxy* sneakers were in there, and two pairs of sneakers that belonged to Tyler.

Her eldest appeared beside her and said with a yawn, "I don't know."

Sam snapped the chest of shoes shut and said, "Well, neither do I." Tyler had a habit of losing things, even things as important to him as his new shoes. He was so little, only eight, but Sam still had a hard time being tolerant of his habitual carelessness. It's not like she was the most organized person in the world—Stacy would be quick to point that out—but she was the one who had to deal with it every time Tyler misplaced something.

He rubbed the sleep from his eyes and cuddled up beside her. "Why do we have to get up so early?"

"It's park day," said Sam, softening. She gathered him into her lap and stroked his disheveled hair. "Don't you want to go to the park?"

"Yeah," whispered Tyler.

He didn't sound thrilled about the prospect. Jasper, on the other hand, was pretty stoked. He came barreling down the hallway wearing plaid shorts, a striped T-shirt, and his *Spider Man* sneakers with no socks. "I'm ready!" he said.

"Me, too," said Sam. "Tyler, will you wear these?" She reached for the black high-tops she'd found in the shoe chest. Tyler shook his head. "OK," she said, "but you have to wear shoes to the park."

Jasper started jumping up and down. "Come on, Mommy!" he yelled.

Sam stood and put her hands on her hips. "We have to find Tyler's shoes."

"They're in our room," said Jasper, still acting like a human po-go stick. Sam headed for the boys' bedroom, with Tyler following close behind. By the time she got to the door he'd passed her and was reaching under the bed for his new sandals like he'd known where they were the whole time.

"Buddy," she said, frowning. She watched as he put on the shoes. They were shiny patent leather, pale pink, and strappy. When they'd gone shopping for them, Sam had suggested that the slip-ons would make life a lot easier, but he'd ignored her and chosen the pair with three buckles on each shoe.

"What's taking so long?" complained Jasper, waving his *Batman* Frisbee in the air. The older kids at the park played Ultimate Frisbee every week, and they'd been kind enough to allow Jasper to play the first time he asked. They used a regulation Frisbee, however, and were a little more serious about points than Jasper wanted to be, so he'd convinced Tarek and a couple of the other kids to start a side game. It had gone well last week, and Jasper was itching to play again.

"Almost ready," said Sam. Tyler was on buckle number four. As he clasped the last two, Sam couldn't help but think how sweet the shoes looked on him. He'd found some fuchsia polish of Stacy's the day before and painted his toenails with it. The bright color was mostly in the right places, although specks of it decorated the soft skin on the top of his feet. The color matched nicely with his new shoes, not quite as well with his green sweat pants, but what did that matter? Stacy, who liked to groom herself and the kids, might have bristled, but as far as Sam was concerned, both boys looked just fine in their self-chosen, self-administered wardrobes.

Tyler stood and Sam breathed a sigh of relief when she saw his smile. The park hadn't been much fun for him lately, and Sam was worried about dragging him somewhere he didn't really want to go. She hoped today would be better than last week, when Willy ran off with the jump rope Tyler had brought. To make matters worse, Max, Alice's huge dog, swiped Tyler's sandwich after he'd taken only one bite. Sam couldn't fathom what a dog would want with a barbecue tempeh burger, and she was right. After snapping it from Tyler's fingers with his large teeth, he'd spit it onto the grass and run off to make some other mischief. Alice apologized, but just barely, and didn't bother reprimanding Willy or leashing Max.

Jasper pulled on Sam's jeans. "Come on, Mommy, come on, come on," he chanted.

"OK," Sam laughed. "Get the cooler."

Jasper appeared beside them with the insulated bag she'd packed with tofu sandwiches, carrot sticks, grapes, and water bottles. "I got it!"

She slung her purse on her shoulder, and Tyler slipped his hand into hers. She squeezed it. "Off we go," she said, opening the door.

They stepped into the bright, beautiful day and headed for the car.

THE park was only a seven minute drive from their condo, but with two bickering boys in the backseat it seemed longer.

"I want it," said Jasper, referring to the plastic microphone Tyler clutched to his chest.

"Nope," said Tyler. "I need it."

"Mama gave it to me," said Jasper. Sam squashed the urge to correct him. Actually, Stacy had given the toy to both of them, but Sam had learned to stay out of their negotiations whenever possible. Tyler was silent and stoic, doing his best imitation of a brick wall. "Come on," pleaded Jasper. "I want to sing."

"I'd love to hear you sing," said Sam, trying to distract Jasper from the quarrel. "How about *Yellow Submarine*?" It worked. Jasper forgot about the microphone and launched into a spirited rendition of his favorite song.

He was just finishing his umpteenth loop of *we all live in a yellow submarine* as Sam pulled into the parking lot. When she peered at her kids in the back seat, Tyler was scowling and covering his ears. Fortunately, Jasper was completely oblivious to that reaction. He finished the song, turned to his brother, and said, "How was that?"

"Awe-some," Tyler said in a put-on husky voice, imitating Stacy when she was psyched about something. Sam smiled. Stacy had been concerned about having their kids so close together, but Sam loved what great friends they were. They had their ups and downs, but really, they were as tight as twins, if completely different from each other. Jasper was a dynamo of energy, Tyler a marvel of sensitivity. Just now, for instance. Sam knew Jasper's singing grated on Tyler, if for no other reason than its decibel level, but he still supported his brother. Her heart swelled with pride at his kindness and emotional intelligence that seemed far beyond his years, but she also worried about how vulnerable that made him, one of the many reasons she was grateful she was homeschooling.

Stacy had been skeptical from day one, and initially only agreed to a trial run. Once they got going, thank goodness, she'd come around to the idea. In the beginning Sam tried school-at-home, mostly at Stacy's insistence, but she and the kids hated it. Jasper, especially, couldn't stay focused on the pre-reading tasks she laid out, or the math activities she sat them down to do every day. He fidgeted and interrupted her constantly, saying he was hungry, or wanted to go out. Tyler sat quietly and said little, but Sam recognized the boredom and disengagement in his blank stare. She decided to switch course and ditched the phonics and flash cards. Before she knew it, they locked into a groove—playing, exploring, and having fun.

Jasper was crazy about bugs, and had taught himself more about ants, beetles, and butterflies than Sam would ever know. It started when he found a click beetle in the sink one morning. That demanded a trip to the library to find out more about beetles and a discussion about whether a beetle is a bug and if not, how can a Junebug be a beetle? Shouldn't it really be called a Junebeetle? A stack of books were checked out and pictures pored over. Bug hunts ensued. An insect zoo was created from jars and tins, complete with an infirmary for injured creatures. The squirmy kid could spend hours stretched out on the ground, armed with a teaspoon of sugar, riveted by the goings on of an anthill. For his birthday he wanted to launch milkweed seeds in their yard in the hopes of attracting monarch butterflies. Not to mention they had found out about a citizen science project tracking the monarch migration to Mexico. Where it would all lead was anyone's guess, but it sure was a fun ride.

Tyler quickly learned to read once she stopped pestering him, and spent much of his time painting elaborate, abstract pictures teeming with geometric shapes and ultra-bright colors, and writing poems about nature in invented spelling. She loved the notes he left around the house for her and Stacy—little love messages on their pillows, Sam's music stand, and Stacy's keyboard. Most of all, she felt grateful her sensitive kid had the space to explore his identity without the pressure he might have felt in a classroom of twenty or more.

Although Sam loved the lifestyle and the opportunity to live and learn with the kids during the brief window of their childhoods, she missed music. There just wasn't enough time or space to gig the way she used to, or write tunes, or even play her trumpet. Teresa and Pina assured her that would change. Sam could already see signs that her kids were becoming less demanding and more self-sufficient about filling their time. Sometimes, she could even practice her horn while they played, even if it was only for short stretches.

Sam tried to talk about her insights and challenges with Stacy, but their conversations always ended up with Sam being the support system for Stacy's worries. As wonderful a wife as Stacy was, she wasn't providing the emotional support Sam needed around the kids and their learning. Thank goodness for the support group and the friends she'd found there.

Sam parked and stepped out of her Subaru as a minivan pulled up beside it. "Hey, Sam!" Teresa rolled down her window to wave.

"Hi!" Sam answered, glad to see Teresa, whom she thought of as the den mother of their little homeschooling pack. She was experienced, level headed, and fun. It was largely because of Teresa—hanging with her at the park, talking to her, and watching her and her kids—that Sam evolved to embrace unschooling.

Teresa had Anthony, Dominic, and Aria with her, and the swarm of kids piled out of her van, most of them heading straight down the hill to the park, waving hello to Sam on their way. Sam opened the back door of her car to let Jasper and Tyler out. Otto, who'd stayed behind, turned to Teresa. "Need any help, Mom?"

"No, thanks, you go ahead. I'll be down in a minute." Otto left and Sam smiled to herself. He was such a mature, smart kid, and a great role model for Tyler and Jasper. She hoped that when they became teens, they'd be a lot like him. "Are you coming over tomorrow night?" Teresa asked.

"Definitely," said Sam. She loved the support group's monthly potlucks. There was always good food, lively conversation, and lots of rambunctiously happy kids. It was also a chance for Stacy to connect with the people Sam spent time with during the day, and that was important to both of them. Sam planned to hit the grocery store later to pick up ingredients for the warm green bean salad she intended to make.

As Tyler and Jasper spilled out of the car, she saw Jasper's face brighten. She turned to see what he was looking at and cringed at the sight of Alice and her brood. "Look what I got!" Willy was racing toward Jasper, waving some sort of electronic device in the air.

He practically skidded to a stop next to Jasper, tossing his prize in the air and catching it on the way down. Sam's gut reaction was to tell him to be careful, but she didn't say anything. Willy wasn't her kid, and Alice, as usual, wasn't paying attention.

"What is it?" asked Jasper excitedly.

"iPhone 6," said Willy.

"Oh," said Jasper without enthusiasm. Sam chuckled inwardly. As far as Jasper was concerned, iPhones were boring things grown-ups used for boring reasons, and Sam and Stacy intended to keep it that way for a while.

"Come on, let's play," said Willy, racing away. Jasper looked at Sam. She nodded and he raced down the hill after Willy.

When Sam turned to take Tyler by the hand and head down to the park with him, she saw that he was talking to Lucy, Alice's little six-year-old. He held out the plastic microphone to her and her eyes lit up as she took it. Before Sam had a chance to enjoy the little bit of sweetness that was happening between the two of them, she got distracted by Alice's big dog.

"No, Max, no!" yelled Teresa, standing between Max and Romeo, her little pug. Max was barking, and Romeo looked to be trembling. Teresa scooped him into her arms and Max started jumping on her. "Stop it, Max!" said Teresa, protectively shielding Romeo.

Alice appeared with Tuck hanging onto her shorts and Silas in her arms. "Come on, Max, don't do that," she said. In Sam's opinion, the reprimand was way too mild. The dog ignored Alice and continued to bark and jump on Teresa. "Max," said Alice, only a smidge more firmly, but at least she had grabbed the dog's collar with her free hand and was pulling him away from Teresa and Romeo.

"Did you bring a leash?" Teresa asked Alice.

"He'll be fine," said Alice, walking away in the direction of the park. Thankfully, Max followed her, but so did Lucy, which Tyler didn't look so happy about.

When she was gone, Sam turned to Teresa and said, "I wish she'd leash him, too. Last week he stole Tyler's sandwich and knocked over some poor toddler."

"I know," said Teresa. "It's maddening."

Tyler was pulling on Sam's jeans, trying to drag her toward the hill. She ignored him for a minute. She didn't want to miss this window. "What can we do about it?"

"I'll talk to her," said Teresa.

Sam wanted to say more, but settled for a simple "Thanks," and walked down the hill with Tyler. As they neared the bottom, he ran ahead to where Lucy was playing on the grass, holding the microphone and singing a song for a group of little girls. Sam was happy to see how much Tyler liked Lucy, she only wished that he and Jasper had picked friends that belonged to someone other than Alice. Oh well, if Teresa could learn to like Alice, she could, too.

The big kids' Frisbee game was in full swing. Jasper, Willy, Tarek and a couple other kids, including Carmen's daughter Anne, were staking out an unused corner of the big field and getting ready to start their game. Sam watched Jasper gesticulating with his little hands, pointing here and there. She hoped he wasn't being too bossy.

Teresa and Carmen and Nasim were standing in a huddle, Carmen crouching to scratch Romeo's ears, Nasim leaning over to tie his sneakers. "Want to walk?" Teresa asked Sam.

"No, thanks," she said. She would have liked nothing more than to do a few loops around the park with the veteran parents, but she felt like she had to keep a close eye on Tyler.

Good thing, too. Teresa and company were barely a quarter of the way into the loop when Sam heard Lucy shrieking. "Give it back," she screamed, holding for dear life onto the plastic mike while Tuck pulled its long, snaky cord.

He was surprisingly strong for a toddler, or else Lucy wasn't pulling back hard enough. The cord's attachment to the mike was tenuous. Severing it would create a whole lot of upset, and there was enough of that already making an appearance on Tyler's frowning, stricken face.

Before Sam could take the ten steps needed to get to him, Tyler had stepped forward and pushed Tuck, who landed with a thump on the grass, his eyes registering wide surprise. Tyler's strategy worked to get Tuck away from the microphone, but it also succeeded in ripping the cord from it. Tuck held the bright red thread of plastic tighter than ever in his tiny fist and let out a blood-curdling screech.

To make matters worse, just as Sam arrived on the scene Max swooped in, snatched the microphone away from Lucy, and ran off with it. Lucy added her screams to Tuck's. Tyler stood in stony silence, but Sam could see his posture sink, his head and shoulders and knees slouching into the position that meant he just wanted to disappear. She kneeled down and hugged him. "I'm sorry, honey," she whispered. She'd talk to him about the pushing later.

Alice arrived with both hands free. A quick glance at the picnic table revealed a delighted Vera, bouncing Silas on her knee. "What happened?" crooned Alice, picking up Tuck.

"He pushed me," Tuck said, hyperventilating between every word and pointing a dirty finger at Tyler.

"Well, that's not nice." Alice glared at Tyler, then at Sam, who felt her blood boil.

"He was trying to get back his toy," she said.

Alice stroked Tuck's hair and looked straight at Tyler when she spoke. "Well, pushing's not OK."

Tyler sank harder into Sam, curling his body tighter, trying to make it smaller. Sam was infuriated now, but she didn't want to make it worse for her son. "Sorry," she said, standing up with Tyler in her arms. He was a tense bundle, his head hanging over her shoulder, his face buried, trying to hide the silent tears she could feel wetting her skin.

Lucy had disappeared. Sam looked around and saw her trying to coax the microphone away from Max. Middle child, dealing. She'd lived that life for most of her childhood. Tuck was still crying, pointing at Tyler with one hand and pulling at Alice's shirt with the other. She ignored his request to nurse, and instead rocked him back and forth, her cheek pressed to his, while shooting dirty looks Sam's way.

She looked like she was about to say something to Sam, but before that could happen Sam walked away fast. She couldn't trust herself to respond civilly, and she needed to attend to Tyler. She found an empty picnic table and sat down. "Hey, buddy," she said, hugging him. "I'm sorry that happened."

He sniffled and looked at her. His face was wet, and a small bit of snot dribbled from his nose. She felt him stiffen. "I hate Tuck," he said.

The declaration made Sam cringe, partly because of the conviction in Tyler's voice and partly because she knew just how he felt. She kept that to herself, and said, "He's just a baby. And you know pushing isn't OK."

Tyler's body relaxed and new tears formed in his eyes. "He wouldn't let go," he said. "Then Max took it."

"I know," said Sam, hugging him close again. "I'm sorry."

Lucy appeared with the microphone. "Tyler," she said. "Look, I got it!" The microphone had been dented, pierced in two places by Max's teeth, and was now without its cord, but Lucy had retrieved it. Tyler peered out from the shelter of his mother's shoulder and looked at Lucy. She stood there grinning and breathless, offering the microphone to him. The corner of his mouth turned up into a small smile. "Come on," said Lucy. "Let's play."

Tyler jumped off Sam's lap and took Lucy's outstretched hand. Sam watched them run, their long hair flying, their laughter mixing with the sounds of birds, the brook, the breeze, and the children, playing.

CHAPTER 9

Pina

Wednesday, June 19

HERE *they come.*

The thought ran through Pina's mind like a mantra, replacing the mantra she'd been trying to drill into her head for the past fifteen minutes. Sam had convinced her to try meditation, to ease some of the anxiety that had come on like gangbusters in mid-life, but Pina felt she was just no good at it, and she wasn't used to feeling like that.

Sam hadn't actually directed any persuasive arguments at Pina directly. She was much too polite for that, and that kind of tactic wouldn't have worked on Pina, anyway. Instead, Sam talked about the benefits of meditation in her own life. It was last week after HoLT's annual Presentation Night, an event which Pina had always loved, but for some reason, this year had gotten on her nerves.

Pina was standing around after the performances with some other moms, and Carmen was talking about her stressful life, which also got on Pina's nerves. Carmen didn't have to work, had three easy peasy girls, and never went out of her way if she could help it, yet somehow she managed to elicit sympathy.

Sam, with a face full of compassion, told Carmen how meditation helped her when she was stressed. Pina listened while downing one of Teresa's peppermint brownies. She could have stuck with the strawberries that Sam was nibbling on, but the sugar seemed to take the edge off her anxiety.

The next day she googled meditation and did a little reading. So far it hadn't helped much. She found it terribly boring, but she was determined to give it more of a chance.

Here they come.

Anthony made it up the stairs first—he always did—and headed straight to his room to do god knew what before book club started. His room was a disaster. Pina had made some half-hearted attempts at trying to get him to clean it, but she gave up pretty quickly and adopted a simple strategy—don't look. It worked as long as Anthony remembered to keep the door closed. That way Pina could avoid seeing the piles of clothes, dishes, books, and papers, but far worse than the mess was the pungent odor emanating from his teenage boy cave.

It was that smell that bothered her most. She knew Anthony wasn't the only one. Teresa told her that she made a point of staying out of Otto's room, too, to steer clear of his sneakers, but Otto was a completely different animal than Anthony—quiet, bookish, brainy. Anthony was full of energy, always needing to move. He exhausted her.

Here they come.

Pina got up from the giant pillow she'd been sitting on as the rest of the kids made their way up the stairs. Seven of them, and they sounded like a herd of elephants. She listened to the din of their loud, happy voices as she rubbed her hip. It was sore. Sitting cross-legged wasn't as easy as it used to be.

Elizabeth had won the race to the coveted seat, the cushy chair in the corner that everyone loved. "Come on, Elizabeth," said Cora. "You sat in it last week."

The rest of the kids made a mad dash for the couch, except for Zoe, who was retrieving the extra chairs they needed from the kitchen, and Isaac, who was setting the snack bag down on the coffee table.

"What is it?" Dominic reached for the bag.

"Uh, uh, uh." Isaac pulled it away. "Not until break."

"Come on Isaac, what's in there?" All of them wanted to know, except for Otto, who sat quietly in the corner, watching the chair scenario unfold.

Elizabeth shrugged her shoulders in a too bad kind of gesture. "I got here first, fair and square."

"It's not fair," fumed Zoe, but she relented and sat next to Cora in one of the kitchen chairs. Pina wondered whether she'd have to do something about the chair situation. She really didn't want to impose seating rules, but it had become an issue.

"OK," she said, taking her designated seat, which was the other cushy chair in the living room. "How was the park?"

"Awesome," said Dominic. "I scored two goals."

"That's because Anthony always passes it to you," said Cora.

Was quiet Cora standing up for herself? That would be a transformation of the kind Pina loved to witness.

Anthony arrived in the living room with what looked like newly combed hair. "I pass to whoever's open," he said.

"You never pass it to the girls," said Zoe.

Anthony laughed nervously, and Dominic joined him, along with Otto. Pina frowned. She didn't always go to Park Day, but when she had she'd noticed the boys had a tendency to monopolize the Frisbee. She'd talked to Anthony and Dominic about it, but apparently there was still a problem, at least as far as Zoe and Cora were concerned.

"OK," said Pina, trying to direct attention to the task at hand. "Let's get started. Otto, who creates the monster?" Pina always started with questions about the book, as a way to make sure the kids read it before the meeting. She was pretty lax about rules, but she refused to allow the sessions to degenerate into a mere social club.

"Victor Frankenstein," he answered.

"Yup," she said. "What about Robert Walton?"

"He's the guy in the beginning," said Dominic.

"He's the Arctic explorer that rescues Victor, and Victor tells him his story," added Zoe. She turned to Dominic. "And he's at the end, too."

"What do you think about using Walton as the frame for the story?" asked Pina.

"It's cool," said Cora, "because you get a different point of view."

"So what do you think of Victor?"

"He's smart," said Elizabeth. "He makes life."

"Actually, he's an asshole." Zoe's answer was swift, and addressed perhaps a little too directly at Elizabeth.

"Whoa, Zoe," said Isaac.

"OK," said Pina. She wasn't going to react to Zoe's language. Making it an issue would just encourage it, and she refused to condescend to the kids. Besides, she didn't really care. She reframed the statement. "Zoe says Victor's a jerk."

"He is kind of a jerk," said Anthony. "But you feel sorry for him."

"I don't feel sorry for him," said Cora. "I feel sorry for the monster."

"The monster is awesome," said Dominic.

And they were off. After an hour of animated discussion Pina felt revitalized. This works way better than meditation, she thought.

"It's snack time," said Dominic.

Pina looked at the clock. "So it is," she said. "Anthony, will you get the cups and water?"

He headed for the kitchen and Zoe followed. "I'll help," she said.

Isaac started unpacking the snack bag. There were organic tortilla chips, a plastic tub filled with homemade salsa, and a batch of cream cheese brownies. "Wow," said Elizabeth. "Nice spread." Isaac smiled.

The subject of food reminded Pina that she had to call Lou and tell him to stop by the Italian market to pick up the sausage she needed for tomorrow night's potluck dish. As if reading her mind, Anthony said to Zoe, "You going to the potluck tomorrow?"

"Course," she said, dipping a chip into the salsa tub.

"It's the June potluck, Anthony," said Elizabeth. "We're all going, duh."

"I can't wait," said Aria, who'd stuck her head in to partake of the snack. "We're bringing mac and cheese."

Otto smiled and looked at Pina. "I love your mac and cheese," he said.

"Thanks," said Pina. "Five minutes and we're back to *Frankenstein*. And save me one of those brownies, OK?"

While they ate, Pina went in the next room and checked her email. Her inbox was ridiculously overstuffed, with HoLT e-list business, messages from new homeschoolers looking for support, announcements for meetings of the town's human rights commission, one from a client, and one from Ellen, who wondered whether Pina could keep Cora for an extra couple of hours until she was done with work. She answered that one in the affirmative and hit delete for most of them, but there were still too many left. They felt like a weight on her shoulders, and she wasn't sure why. She'd always been a doer, and she'd always loved having her fingers in a million pies.

Was it some kind of midlife crisis? She wasn't sure. Anthony was becoming more independent every day, and Dominic wasn't far behind. Aria had turned ten this year, and Pina missed having little ones.

She closed her eyes, took a deep breath, and listened. She heard chips crunching, kids talking, and lots of laughter.

She smiled.

LOU forgot the sausage. "Seriously? Now I have to go to the supermarket myself."

"I'll go," said Lou. "What else do we need?"

Pina still felt annoyed, but it was hard to be mad at Lou when he was being so nice. He was always nice, but sometimes Pina found herself being mad at him, anyway. She knew her feelings weren't his fault, but she'd always had a hard time controlling her emotions. Her friends thought she was passionate and outspoken. The people she'd alienated with her bluntness didn't put it so kindly.

Of course she didn't expect everyone to like her, but it bothered her, for instance, that Carmen was more popular than she was. At least that's what it felt like to Pina. Teresa disagreed, and said it wasn't that people didn't like Pina, it was more like they admired her and were maybe a little intimidated by her. Maybe some people, but Pina knew that wasn't the case with everyone. Pina had a knack for understanding interpersonal dynamics and other people's motivations. She also had a difficult time holding her tongue about those things, but she never meant to be mean, just honest. Carmen, on the other hand, could pile on the bullshit so thick that Pina had to walk away before saying something inappropriate. It irked Pina to no end that people would rather be coddled than deal with a straight shooter.

"Mom?" Aria stuck her head into the kitchen, where Pina was perusing the contents of the refrigerator. "Can I go to Anne's house to watch a movie after dinner?"

"You'll walk there?"

"Yes," said Aria.

"What movie?"

"Pride and Prejudice."

"How will you get home?"

"Can you pick me up?"

Pina spied a container of sauce. Bingo. "Sure," she said. "Want to help with dinner?"

"OK," said Aria, grabbing an apron.

"Chop some carrots and onions and celery," said Pina. "And let's throw in some chard."

"What are we making?"

"A chicken thing," said Pina.

"Mom," said Aria as she peeled the carrots. "Who do you think wrecked Tarek's dinosaur?"

"Is he still upset about that?"

"I don't know," said Aria.

Pina's antennae quivered. "Why do you ask?"

"Carmen was talking about it," said Aria.

"Figures," said Pina. "I'm sure it wasn't malicious, just some kid wanting to play. Whoever it was liked the dinosaur. It's a compliment."

Aria laughed. "Carmen thinks it was Tuck."

"And if it was?" said Pina. "He's two, for Christ sake."

"He got chocolate on the piano keys."

Pina finished transferring the chicken legs into a cast iron pan, washed her hands, and turned to Aria. "Is Carmen talking about that, too?"

"Anne told me," she said.

"Don't you two have anything better to talk about?" Aria looked at the floor. "Hey," said Pina, giving her a hug. "Toddlers are active. They get into things. You should have seen your brothers." Pina changed the subject to the vegetable garden. "Go pick some radishes and lettuce," she said, and Aria went outside.

Once the chicken, veggies, sauce, and spices were simmering, Pina went to see what the boys were up to. She didn't have to go far before she heard the sounds of music wafting from upstairs. Anthony was playing his bass, and Dominic was sawing away at his fiddle. Anthony played electric at Otto's house, with a couple of kids that Otto met at a rock and roll camp he'd gone to, but Pina was glad that at home they stuck to acoustic music.

She went back to the kitchen, peered out the window, and saw that Aria had been sidetracked in the backyard by the bunnies. That was fine, the salad would only take a minute and the chicken wouldn't be ready for a while. Pina picked up the phone and dialed. Carmen answered on the second ring.

"Hi," said Pina.

"Hey, Pina," said Carmen in her usual cheerful tone. "What's up?"

"Just checking in," she said. "Aria says she's walking to your house after dinner to watch *Pride and Prejudice*."

"Great," said Carmen. "I'm making popcorn. You should come, too."

"I've already seen it," said Pina, "I have a ton of stuff to do."

"OK," said Carmen. "You're going to the potluck tomorrow, right?"

"Of course," said Pina, and paused. "I heard you're still annoyed about Tarek's dinosaur."

"Oh, that," said Carmen. "I'm sure he can make another one, I just wish Alice would watch her kids."

"We don't know that it was Tuck," said Pina.

"You said his name," said Carmen. "I didn't. But let's face it, he's into everything."

"He's two," said Pina. "And Alice has a baby. Give her a break."

"I'll give her a break," said Carmen, "but that doesn't mean I have to like it."

"Well, stop talking about it in front of the kids. They don't need to hear it." Pina felt that familiar silence on the other end of the phone that happened in so many of her conversations. "Carmen?"

"I'm here," she said. "We'll see Aria in a couple hours, then?"

"Yes," said Pina.

They hung up, and Pina got the rice going.

DINNER was delicious, even Anthony commented on it, and Lou, bless his heart, had picked up Pina's favorite cherry pie at the supermarket along with the sausage and a gallon of milk.

It put Pina in a good mood and gave her plenty of energy to spend the evening writing an article about the upcoming speaker the human rights commission was sponsoring in August. She got the save-the-date notice sent out to the list, and even had time to clear out more of her inbox, which included writing back to a couple of newbies asking questions about homeschooling, as well as doing some research on finding a new campsite for HoLT's annual trip right after Labor Day.

She was breathing easy when she got in the Corolla a little after ten to drive to Carmen's house. It was a lovely night, the first of several in the forecast.

Carmen lived close to Pina, but on a much quieter, dead end street, in a much bigger house. Pina pulled to the side of the road and took a deep breath, smelling the sweet June air. Anthony's community college class was done, Aria's dance was finished for the year, Dominic's violin teacher was on hiatus until August, and there was one more week of book group before most of their scheduled activities ended. The boys would play Frisbee and their musical instruments and go sailing, and she and Aria would make jam and tend the garden. They'd all hang out at the beach with their friends, read books, and go to outdoor concerts and plays. She was glad it was summer.

As she got out of the car she looked through the living room window to see Carmen and Emma snuggling on the couch next to a giant bowl. Lizzie and Anne and Aria would be stretched out on the floor in a big cuddly heap. No sounds came from the house save those from the movie, Darcy and Elizabeth cementing their happily ever after. Pina felt a surge of gratitude, and wondered whether the meditation was kicking in, after all.

She stayed outside in the still, perfect night for a few minutes, until she heard the credits rolling, then rang the doorbell to be invited in for hugs, leftover popcorn, and a long chat with Carmen before collecting Aria and heading home.

CHAPTER 10

Dogs and Park Day

Wednesday, June 19

From: StacyParsons
Sent: 6/19/2015 6:03 PM
To: HoLT
Subject: [HoLT] Dogs and park day

Hi Everyone,

Stacy here. Sam and I are looking forward to seeing
everyone at the June potluck. I understand from Sam that
people might continue going to the park over the summer,
too, which sounds great! One concern I have is that some
people have been bringing unleashed dogs. Some dogs
are actually bigger than some of the kids, and have been
scaring them, stealing their lunches, and otherwise
detracting from their socialization experiences. Can we
all remember to be respectful and leash our dogs?

Thanks,
Stacy

From: PinaAndCompany
Sent: 6/19/2015 7:13 PM
To: HoLT
Subject: Re: [HoLT] Dogs and park day

I haven't been to park day in a while, my kids go with
Teresa. She always leashes Romeo, so I know she's not the
culprit. Maybe those who are bringing unleashed dogs can
be spoken to directly?

Pina

From: EllenRutherford
Sent: 6/19/2015 7:48 PM
To: HoLT
Subject: Re: [HoLT] Dogs and park day

I think leashing dogs is a good idea. It's also part of town
regulations.

Ellen

From: AliceBillKids
Sent: 6/19/2015 8:22 PM
To: HoLT
Subject: Re: [HoLT] Dogs and park day

I try to keep Max leashed whenever possible but sometimes
he just needs to run. I'll try and keep a closer eye on him.

Alice

From: StacyParsons
Sent: 6/19/2015 8:33 PM
To: HoLT
Subject: Re: [HoLT] Dogs and park day

Hi Alice,

I understand that Max needs to run but he does disturb the little kids, steal their food, etc. Can he get his exercise at a time other than park day?

Thanks, Stacy

From: TereesieE
Sent: 6/19/2015 9:12 PM
To: HoLT
Subject: Re: [HoLT] Dogs and park day

Hi Everyone,

This is a good discussion. I just talked with Alice on the phone. Max will be leashed at the park from now on. See you all at my house tomorrow!

Teresa

CHAPTER 11

Nasim

Thursday, June 20

CRADLING the hot cup in his hands, Nasim crossed the living room and perched on the edge of the glider. Dust danced in the morning sunlight. He set his cup down and reached to open the window, letting in the scent of fresh cut grass and the sound of birdsong. He removed the tea bag and set it on one of the dishes that hadn't made its way to the kitchen yet, propping his feet on the coffee table and settling in with his laptop to finish reading *The Atlantic* article he had started last night. Tarek was still sleeping and this was his time.

"Nasim! What are you making to bring to the potluck tonight?" Sarah yelled from her office down the hall. Nasim cringed, hoping she hadn't woken Tarek.

"Hmm? What potluck?"

He looked up to see her leaning in the doorway, holding her cup of coffee. "Seriously? We just talked about this last night. Teresa and Russell are hosting. I assumed you would be taking care of what dish to bring."

"Oh right. Well, Tarek and I are headed to the farm this afternoon, so I figured I'd work in a trip to the grocery store on the way home and pick up some chips and salsa."

"Nasim. We cannot bring that to the potluck. It's just not respectful. I know local veggies aren't plentiful this time of year, but there's got to be something yummy and wholesome you can make from scratch."

Nasim saw the fantasy of his calm, self-paced day slip away from him. Instead of finishing the article, rousing Tarek, and enjoying some putter time around the house before heading out to work at the farm this afternoon, he was going to have to figure out what to make, and worse, get the ingredients. "Any ideas?" he asked Sarah, hopefully.

"Well, it's not exactly local, but it is gluten-free and vegan if you make homemade hummus and bring fresh vegetables to dip. Maybe some olives, too."

He knew there was no point in arguing. With all the work Sarah put into supporting local, organic agriculture, she wouldn't be able to show her face if they arrived at the potluck with store bought chips and salsa. Thinking ahead to the appreciative smiles and bowl scraped clean at the potluck ("Nasim, *you* made this?") he put his tea and computer down, and roused himself from his chair.

"All right. But if you want me to fit that in, I'm going to run to the store now and get the ingredients while Tarek is still sleeping. I won't have time to get everything done otherwise."

"Well, you would have if you had thought ahead a little. I don't think it's fair to put it on me. But fine. I have a conference call in an hour, so don't take too long."

Nasim threw on his sweatshirt and grabbed his keys from the counter, letting the screen door slam behind him. In the car, he switched from Sarah's favorite NPR station to a podcast of the Newport Folk Festival. He backed out of the driveway, rolled down the window, and took off. He wondered what it would be like if he were the one making the money and Sarah were the one who had primary kid duty. Sometimes he got self-conscious about being a full-time dad. And let's face it, a homeschooling full-time dad. Talk about fringe. But most days he was glad it had worked out this way. When he got laid off he hadn't realized how the lack of income would be offset by the time spent with Tarek and the friendships he'd form. They were a definite improvement from the banter-around-the-water-cooler type contacts he'd had at work. He knew he was lucky to be able to spend time with other families who had chosen this lifestyle. And he knew Sarah was right, as usual— the potluck was something worth putting more effort into than store bought chips and dip. Most of the families they'd be breaking bread with were an integral part of his life.

HIS mind wandered to the museum trip last week. He remembered "field trips" when he was a kid. Not too much about any of the trips actually. For him they were a get-out-of-school free card. Just not having to be in school was what was good about them, a change in routine. Still, the class was shuffled from one exhibit to the next and talked at by the teacher. The good part was at least you were moving around and could talk to your friends.

On the drive there, Nasim had asked Tarek if he wanted to start at a particular area of the museum. Tarek said he'd like to check out the math exhibit, then go see the live animals.

They'd met up with Carmen and her girls in the lobby. Carmen had gotten a special group rate for the visit. "Nasim! Tarek! Great to see you guys. We're just waiting for a couple of other families and then we'll go in together. How have you been? How's Sarah?"

"Working hard as usual. How about Henry?"

"He's out of town again. So anyway, Elizabeth is dying to go through the special exhibit on the Maya."

"Tarek wanted to browse the math exhibit."

Anne and Emma tugged at Carmen's hands. "Mom, can we go with Nasim and Tarek instead? Pleeeease?"

Carmen looked up to question Nasim.

"Sure," he said. Let's meet up in an hour or so at the live animals exhibit."

"Great idea. Everyone?" She raised her voice to gain the attention of the assembled homeschoolers. "We're ready to go in now. Enjoy yourselves, and if you want, we're going to regroup at about noon at the live animal exhibit." She thanked Nasim and admonished Anne and Emma, "Girls, you stick with Nasim and don't give him any trouble."

They all single filed through the turnstile before splintering off. Carmen and Elizabeth headed to the third floor for the special exhibit, while Nasim, Tarek, Anne, and Emma made a left to the math section.

On entering the room, the kids scattered, each to examine a different interactive exhibit. Nasim wandered between them, observing, answering questions, and reading instructions when asked. A lot of his enjoyment came from watching how the kids approached the museum. This kind of absorption must be what museum designers fantasize about when they create exhibits. Every once in a while one would call the others over to share a discovery and the sound of appreciative "oohs" and "ahs" filled the room.

When Alice and her gang of four—oops now five—joined them, the sharing and excitement continued. Tarek pulled Alice's oldest, Isaac, over to show him the Mobius strip, and Isaac gladly followed. He was three years older than Tarek, but neither of them found anything wrong or weird about a younger child being friends with, or even teaching, an older one. And there was ten-year-old Anne, lifting Alice's two-year-old, Tuck, up to get a better look, too.

Alice leaned against a bar while the baby nursed. Nasim didn't know how she managed with five. He felt his hands were full with one, but maybe in some ways having siblings around made life easier. Sarah worried about Tarek having enough opportunities to interact with other kids. Nasim wasn't too concerned about it. It seemed to him that learning how to be alone was a valuable skill, but to keep the peace he did make an effort to have friends over. And of course it didn't hurt that when Tarek was invited to a friend's house as often happened after an outing like this, Nasim got some free time. No one kept a tally, but it seemed to work out pretty evenly. He knew there were some families with more formal arrangements, but Nasim was happy with the organic nature of his child swapping.

He pulled his phone out of his pocket to check the time. "Alice, are you planning to meet up with the rest of the gang at the live animals?"

"Sure, I guess so. If the kids want to."

"OK, I'll corral them." He went over to where Tarek and some others were huddled together. "Guys, five minutes and we're heading down to the live animals to meet up with Carmen and whoever else."

The kids straggled out of the math exhibit, forming an amoeba-like shape that changed as kids switched position to walk with one person, then another. Nasim didn't need to direct them—they were regulars at the museum. He and Alice followed. Again he compared it to his own museum going experience as a kid. It seemed like the goal used to be to rush through as many exhibits as possible, never spending a significant amount of time in any one place. I guess they were trying to get their money's worth. Tarek was able to discover new spaces and return to old as his curiosity drove him. And the great thing was that with the cheaper rate, they could afford to come frequently. Thank goodness for people like Carmen who seemed game to organize these things on a regular basis.

Entering the live animal hall, he saw kids buzzing around, some focused on the animal exhibits, others chatting together. He and Alice joined the moms stationed near the doorway. "So, what's the plan after this?" asked Carmen. "Are people eating lunch here or what?"

"I'm flexible," said Nasim. "I didn't pack anything but I'm not opposed to buying something in the cafeteria."

Carmen seemed a little frazzled. "Hmm. I packed some snacks from home. I hope if my girls see other kids buying the junk they sell here, they won't bug me for it."

Nasim kept his mouth shut. Alice piped up, "I brought snacks too. Maybe we can get a table together, Carmen."

Sam settled it. "I'm starved. Let's head up."

At the cafeteria, Carmen and Alice grabbed a table by the windows and started doling out food. Nasim and Tarek got in line to get slices. Carrying their trays into the noisy room, they found their friends and sat down, Tarek with the kids, Nasim with the moms.

Nasim turned to Teresa. "Hey, I haven't seen you yet today. What's up?"

"Cora's with us today."

Nasim glanced at Otto and Cora sitting at the kids' table, and his eyes narrowed with interest.

"I know nothing!" Teresa exclaimed, throwing her hands up in response to his stare. "Anyway, we went straight to the Maya exhibit. It was awesome."

After lunch, Tarek said he wanted to go check out the Maya exhibit since Otto had given it good reviews. Thanking Carmen for organizing, they headed out.

ONE good thing about going to the grocery store at ten a.m. on a Thursday morning: plenty of parking spaces. He knew it was best to get this shopping trip out of the way, but he missed having Tarek along. He really was a help. The kid got such a kick out of choosing vegetables and weighing them. Just a couple weeks ago he had noticed "unit pricing" and was on a roll of figuring out what was the best buy. Of course this started a conversation about you get what you pay for, and Nasim had showed him how to find ingredients on the labels. Needless to say, with Sarah as a mom, Tarek was pretty in tune with what foods are good for you and what not so good. At least according to her. Nasim knew that asking one of the other families would elicit a very different opinion. Food could be like a religion to some people.

In the checkout line Nasim kicked himself for having forgotten the reusable bags. Sarah always kept one in her backpack, but Nasim had to just try to consolidate everything into as few bags as possible.

At home, it was quiet. After depositing the bags on the kitchen counter, he poked his head into Sarah's office to see her bring her finger to her lips. Her headset was on and she was in the middle of the conference call. Could Tarek still be sleeping? He cracked open his bedroom door and spotted him in a sea of Legos, a mostly-empty cereal bowl beside him. The CD player was loaded with whatever story Tarek was in the middle of, probably one he'd listened to a hundred times before, and he was searching for a specific Lego piece. He was so engrossed he didn't hear his dad.

Nasim left the door cracked open, and went to put away the groceries. He decided to make the hummus now. That way he wouldn't have to rush home from the farm later. There wouldn't be enough time to use dried beans, so he'd gotten canned. He remembered how his mother always left the tahini out when she made it, and doubled up on the lemon, but Nasim loved sesame and had long since revised her recipe. Never in question was using plenty of garlic. He assembled the food processor, plugged it in, and started mixing.

"Dad! Look what I made!" Nasim looked up to see Tarek slide into the kitchen in his socks. The grinding noise of the food processor must have roused him from his room. He carried his latest creation, some kind of futuristic dinosaur, and zoomed it around Nasim, looking hungrily at the hummus.

"Lunch?"

"No buddy. This is for the potluck at Otto and Vera's later. We do need to eat though, before we head over to the farm today. And where's that cereal bowl Tarek?"

"Aww Dad do we have to go? I'm in the middle of building another Deinonychus and I don't feel like it."

"Yes actually, we do have to go. We made a commitment. So go put some shoes on, and grab that cereal bowl. Then you and I will eat and head out. Bring a book in case it's slow. I'll pack the sketching stuff and a snack."

He watched his son slump down the hall to his room. He knew it was hard to tear away from the morning's activity, but it would be good to move around, get outside, and see friends after lunch.

Nasim garnished the hummus as his mother would have, drizzling some olive oil over the top, scattering a few whole chick peas and olives across it, a sprinkle of sumac and a little parsley, for color. He packed it up, along with some vegetables and Syrian bread for dipping. He'd made a double batch, so there should be plenty in case there were hordes of people tonight. Even if there weren't hordes, the teenagers alone could really put it away.

For lunch he scraped out the remains of the last couple nights' dinners into a pan, and set it over low heat. He threw in some butter, an egg for protein, and mixed it around. When the egg set, he called it done and spooned it out into two bowls.

Tarek slouched into the kitchen, shoes untied, still carrying his Lego dinosaur. Nasim set Tarek's lunch on the table and handed him a fork.

"What is it Dad?"

"Let's call it Surprise Supreme! Would you like a little cheese grated on top?"

Tarek gave Nasim a withering look and shrugged his shoulders. "Sure I guess. How old are the leftovers?"

"Oh not so old. Just from the past couple days. I wanted to use them up since we'll be going to the potluck for dinner tonight."

Tarek brightened. "Oh yeah! I can show Otto my dino! Is it OK if I bring it Dad?"

"Sure. As long as you're OK with it possibly getting destroyed over the course of the night. Now eat up. We don't want to be late for our shift."

Tarek scooped with one hand, while the other maneuvered the dinosaur to explore the kitchen table, sometimes mounting a surprise attack on Nasim's dish from above. Apparently the destruction of his Presentation Night dinosaur a week ago hadn't left a scar. Nasim credited himself with de-escalating that situation. Sarah had wanted to find the culprit, but Nasim had convinced her there was no point in crying over spilt milk, and after all, Legos were designed to be taken apart and put back together. With a room full of kids, it was almost impossible to imagine it not happening over the course of the night.

When Nasim and Tarek finished lunch, Nasim put the dishes in the sink, and then remembered that he hadn't seen Tarek's cereal bowl make its way in yet.

"Tarek, you clear the dishes from your room. I'm going to do a sweep of the rest of the house before we go." On his way back to the kitchen, carrying his now cold cup of tea, he poked his head into Sarah's office. "Any dirty dishes for me? I'm cleaning up and then we're heading to the farm." Sarah handed him her coffee cup from the morning.

"Thanks. What time will you guys be back?"

"Not sure. Our shift is over at 4:30, but we might stay later or stop at the library on the way home. What time do you want to get to the potluck?"

"Let's aim for 6:30." She turned back to her computer, and he headed to the kitchen with the dishes.

Sarah was driven. She didn't have a lot of discretionary time to spend with Nasim and Tarek. One of the downsides to working primarily from home—you were always at work. Nasim would have liked more time together, but he could hardly fault her when she was making the money that allowed him to be at home with Tarek. It did irk him, though, that she couldn't seem to really trust him with the job one hundred percent. When they had discussed it, it had made sense for her to take on the money-making role. He was burned out at his job and when he got laid off, she was glad for the opportunity to take on more responsibility at her job, working for a cause she was passionate about. But having been the one "in charge" of Tarek, it sometimes seemed to him that she still wanted to be, or didn't trust him to do it to her satisfaction. Or maybe it was just some regret on her part that she wasn't doing it anymore. And maybe partly it was his own doubts and anxieties that were surfacing. So he didn't bring it up. In any case, it didn't seem like Tarek was suffering at all. He had adapted to the new configuration.

And really, Sarah and Nasim were well suited to their current roles. Sarah had always been goal oriented, passionate, and a bit of a workaholic. Nasim was more laid back and able to go with the flow. He thought he'd ease back into the world of outside employment when Tarek got a little older, but this felt right for now.

Dishes soaking, bag packed, Nasim and Tarek headed out to the farm. This was one way Nasim could contribute to the finances and keep Tarek with him. In exchange for working the distribution once a week for the CSA, their family got a discounted summer share of produce. Nasim always made sure Tarek brought a book or some other activity along to occupy him, but in practice, he always ended up having more fun doing Nasim's job with him. Greeter extraordinaire, he met each shareholder at the door with a smile, and shouted their name out to be checked off the list by Nasim. If it wasn't too busy, he did this part himself, scrolling through the names in alphabetical order and then sliding across the grid to mark off the appropriate week. He usually had some tips to offer about the pick-your-own crop of the week, and gave directions on how to find it. "Go back past the greenhouse and then you'll see the signs near the herbs." After Nasim carried out a box of produce to refill, Tarek was happy to arrange the vegetables artistically, and sometimes tried his hand at sketching a still life. The most exciting part for Tarek was if someone decided to purchase something from the farm stand. This meant ringing it into the cash register, and figuring out the change to hand over.

At the end of the shift, when Nasim was cleaning up and making sure everything was in order, Tarek would go out to the fields. Nasim often found him on his stomach, nose to the ground, examining some creature or new shoot at close range, or helping another shareholder navigate the crops, or asking the farmer questions. Even on the rainy days, provided he'd remembered his boots, Tarek was happy to spend time exploring. Nasim and Sarah were glad he had this hands-on connection to where his food came from. It was important to both of them.

When it was time to go home, Nasim and Tarek stomped the mud off their boots and climbed into the car. "Tarek, I'm going to stop by the library to return some books, but we can't stay long— I've got to get home in time to take a shower before the potluck tonight."

"OK Dad."

"We can look for about ten minutes. That's all."

"OK."

At the library Tarek ran down the stairs to the Children's Department and went straight to the desk. "Is Jill here?" he asked the teenager who was shifting books from one cart to another.

"She's in the back. Hold on I'll get her."

Jill poked her head around the corner. "Hey champ! I thought I heard you. How's it going, Tarek? Did you finish *The Lightning Thief?*"

"Yeah, I actually listened to it twice. I want to get the next one now, and also some books on Greek gods and goddesses."

Jill and Tarek headed off to the stacks, each as excited as the other by their mutual love of the novel.

Nasim scanned the activity calendar while he waited. He was glad to see how comfortable Tarek was with the librarian, and how he saw her as an ally. There were adults besides him and Sarah that Tarek could depend on and learn from, especially when it came to things like fantasy novels where Nasim's expertise was a little lacking. He made a mental note to ask Tarek if he was interested in signing up for the beginning chess class when registration opened.

Jill and Tarek emerged with a stack of books. "Jill says I can take as many as I can carry Dad! Thanks Jill!" He grinned up at her.

"OK buddy. Time to go."

At the circulation desk, Tarek made a show of unloading his armload on the desk. "Dad, can we use your card? I don't know where mine is."

The circulation assistant raised her eyebrows at the stack of books on Greek mythology. "You have a paper due for school?"

"No," said Tarek.

The woman looked confused. "Then why are you taking out so many books?"

"Because I'm interested in them?" Tarek queried back.

"Oh! That's a good reason I guess!" she said, as she took Nasim's card to check them out.

Nasim kicked himself for the second time that day for forgetting a bag. Oh well, he and Tarek could share the load. But leaving the library, Tarek insisted he could carry them all. "Remember what Jill said!" he quipped and happily struggled back to the car, laden with his pile of beloved reading material.

At home Nasim glanced at the clock and saw he would have to move swiftly if he wanted to accomplish all he'd planned and leave for the potluck on time. Well, maybe the dishes were just going to have to wait until tomorrow. He yelled to Sarah that they were home and went to jump in the shower. The day hadn't gone exactly as he'd planned, but so far it had turned out pretty well. Turning the water off, he grabbed a towel and dripped down the hall to find Sarah, still glued to her desk.

"Hey," he said, bending over and giving her a kiss.

"Hey to you!" she kissed him back. "You got me wet!"

Nasim winked.

Sarah rolled her eyes. "Is it time to go? Is the hummus ready? Does Tarek need a shower before we leave? Did you remember to return the overdue library books?

"Yes, yes, no and yes. I'm pretty sure Tarek will end up outside at Teresa's tonight, so we might as well hold off on the shower until bedtime. I'm going to get dressed and then we should head out."

Stopping by Tarek's room, Nasim saw he had already popped the CD from the sequel into the player and was settling into his Legos. "Bud, remember we're going out?"

"Oh yeah! I'm going to see Otto. Got to bring the dino."

"OK we're leaving in five." Stepping on a Lego on his way out, Nasim winced and turned around. "Time to clear a path through these blocks. They've become a hazard."

In his room Nasim pulled on clean pants and a shirt and headed to the kitchen, where Sarah and Tarek were waiting, munching on carrot sticks. Tarek was telling Sarah about his afternoon. Nasim retrieved the carrot sticks from them.

"Hey, those are for the potluck you guys." He nabbed the hummus from the fridge, along with the olives, more vegetables, and bread. He dangled the keys in front of Sarah. "You can drive."

Tarek was already out the door, dino appearing to lead the way. Sarah followed, "You can finish telling me what happened in the car!" she yelled at his back. "Are you sure you want to bring that dinosaur?"

Nasim smiled, pulling the door closed behind him.

CHAPTER 12

Alice

Thursday, June 20

FLOORBOARDS creaking, doorknob rattling, a streak of sunlight across the bed. Alice opened her eyes to see the silhouette of her husband Bill. He squatted down to nuzzle Silas, and then Alice's neck. Alice inhaled the smell of Bill mixed with aftershave. Silas was still latched but his strong sucking had changed to the intermittent fluttering that signaled he was drifting back to sleep.

"Time?" Alice said.

"Yup. The gang's all fed. I'm heading out."

Alice reached for his tie and held him a moment longer. "Remember tonight is the potluck at Teresa and Russell's. Do you want us to wait for you to go, or meet us there?"

"I better meet you there. I might get off a little late tonight." Alice pulled him in closer for a kiss. "Uh oh. Does that mean I'll miss all the food?" he said, standing up.

"I'll save you a plate. We're going to make lasagne."

"Mmmm. My favorite. I'll be dreaming about it all day. See you later. Love you." He leaned over to kiss her again and ran his hand over Silas's bald head.

As he headed out the door, Alice broke Silas's latch with her pinky and held him to her as she sat up. She could hear the sounds of the other kids saying their goodbyes to Bill. Alice stuck her feet in her slippers and made her way out to the kitchen. Still holding Silas, she grabbed the sling from the hook by the door and nestled him into it. She poured herself a cup of coffee and took it to the couch in the adjacent family room. As soon as her rear hit the cushion, Tuck's mommy milk radar went off. He climbed up and asked for "other side milk."

Alice cuddled him in close and pretended to eat him up. "Nom nom nom you are delicious. Remember we talked about how other side milk is for Silas in the day, but you can have yours before bed?" Tuck's face started to crumple. "Let's read a book instead. You pick."

Tuck shakily inhaled, holding back tears and sliding off the couch in slow motion. Settling himself on the floor next to the bookcase, he began pulling out one book after another.

Isaac sat at the piano practicing. Alice was glad he seemed to do it with no prodding. Not so Willy and Lucy. With the lesson later today, she wondered how much they had really applied themselves. Part of her felt that if they were paying for the lessons, then the kids should put the time in to practice. Another part of her thought maybe the lessons were of value in and of themselves. Conflicted, she hung in the middle, didn't push for the most part, and then on lesson day got anxious that their teacher, Kevin, would be frustrated by their lack of progress.

"Willy, have you practiced at all this week?"

"Some, Mom," Willy let out under his breath.

"Because Kevin is coming today."

Willy was engrossed in his computer game, and Lucy was watching his every move.

Alice reflected on how each child had approached the home-school Presentation Night last week. There had been a lot of kids (and even Jewel) who had a talent or accomplishment to share.

Isaac had played *Für Elise* and one of his own compositions on the piano. Afterwards, he decided that it was fun to have a set goal and thought he'd participate in a recital if Kevin organized one. Willy was supposed to prepare Bastian's *Tarantello,* but had made a strong case for bringing along some of the pottery he had made on the wheel in his homeschoolers' pottery class instead. Alice thought possibly he preferred not to compete with his brother in the realm of piano, and in any case his interests seemed to lay elsewhere, right now largely in the world of *Minecraft.* Alice had been concerned that Lucy's lack of piano practice would only lead to embarrassment, so she hadn't officially signed her up to do anything. But when Lucy saw the crowd, there was nothing she wanted more than to perform for them, so Carmen had let her go after Isaac, and to Lucy's credit, she had pulled off a pretty nice rendition of *Twinkle Twinkle Little Star,* even singing along. It was almost as if having an audience honed her skill. And then Tuck! Seeing his sister on stage and hearing "Tinkle Tinkle" had propelled him off Alice's lap, across the room, half of his brownie smeared on face and hands, half trailed Hansel-and-Gretel-style on the floor behind him. On the stage he ran up and down in front of the piano, alternately banging the keys and running trills, wearing his chocolate grin. Alice smiled at the memory. He just wanted so badly to keep up with the big ones.

Alice's gaze settled on the dog, sprawled contentedly in a pool of sunlight. "Did anyone take Max out this morning?"

Isaac turned his head toward her. "Dad did."

"When Isaac's done, why don't each of you review what Kevin said you were supposed to work on this week," Alice suggested to Willy and Lucy's backs.

Tuck handed up three books, and climbed back on the couch. Alice began to read. Lucy wandered over and settled herself next to Tuck.

"Lucy, do you want to read to Tuck, too? We can take turns."

"Yes, mommy." Alice listened and Tuck turned the pages as Lucy "read" *Knuffle Bunny*. She pretty much knew this book by heart so Alice didn't think too much phonetic sounding out of words was happening, but she knew from Isaac that this memorization and reciting was part of how they learned to read independently. Isaac had been read to, had free access to books, and had enjoyed word games and invented spelling. Observing his progress, she offered him a simple chapter book when he was six, and to his own amazement, he was able to read it!

When Willy was six he announced that he wanted to learn how to read. Whatever he meant by it, Alice's schooled brain took it to mean phonetics, and she instituted a regimen of ten minutes a day "teaching" Willy to read. Those two weeks stood out for both of them as some of the roughest in their relationship. A lesson presumably mastered one day was apparently forgotten the next. Had he really forgotten? Or was he purposely pushing her buttons to get out of the activity that he had requested? If she stopped, was that teaching him to give up if something didn't come easily? When reviewing the letter "e" left both of them in tears one day, the light bulb switched on. Alice told Willy she was done with the reading lessons, and he could let her know if he wanted to resume. What followed were a couple years of lots of books on tape, being read to nightly, word games, and then, voila! At eight, Willy was reading independently, just like Isaac had at six. His timeline was just different.

As they came to the end of the third book, Alice closed the cover and finished her coffee. Silas had awoken and latched on again.

"All right, everybody. Time to get dressed. Kevin will be here in fifteen minutes." Alice got off the couch and took Lucy and Tuck by the hand.

"Lucy, put something on that will be good to play outdoors in later." Last week it had worked pretty well to go for a run while the older kids were having their lesson, and Alice planned to do it again this week. As long as Willy and Lucy had their lessons first, Isaac was available to hold down the fort while she was gone, and she would time it to be back before it was his turn for a lesson.

In her room, Alice put Silas on the bed, and Tuck climbed up next to him. Silas squealed with glee as his big brother made faces at him. Alice grabbed her running clothes from the closet, all the while keeping an eye on the bed. When the inevitable happened, and Tuck's fun face-making escalated to a more frenzied level of play that put Silas at risk of being bounced off the bed, she picked Silas up and told Tuck to come along. Hearing the bell, he jumped down and raced to the front door. Lucy, barefoot but dressed in flowered leggings, a sweatshirt, and hair pulled into several random ponytails, had beat him to it. She swung open the door and jubilantly greeted Kevin.

Thank goodness for Kevin. So far at least he seemed able to meet each of the kids where they were. Maybe having home-schooled himself made him more open to the variations in their learning styles, and their levels of commitment to piano. He tossed his bag on the sofa and grinned.

"Who's up first today?"

"I thought it worked out OK last week leaving Isaac in charge when I went for a run. What would you think if I do it again?"

"Sure, that should be fine."

"I'll have my cell phone with me. Isaac, you can text me, but only if it's something really important, OK?"

"Sure, Mom."

Alice surveyed the situation and saw that Willy hadn't gotten dressed and was still playing his computer game.

"Looks like Lucy's first today." Alice crouched next to Willy. Under her breath she said, "Remember I said fifteen minutes twenty minutes ago? Come on—you need to get dressed." She waited for a response but none came. "Willy! I'm talking to you."

"OK, OK, I'm just finishing this."

"Time's up. No gaming while piano lessons are happening. Go get some clothes on."

Willy swiveled on the chair and slouched toward his room. Alice felt the heat rising in her face. Sometimes it seemed like Willy just tuned her out. She wasn't sure if it was the power of his concentration, or whether he was deliberately ignoring her when she needed him to do something he didn't feel like doing.

Alice powered off the computer, gave Isaac the thumbs up, grabbed a bag of goldfish and a sippy cup for Tuck and went out the back door, holding it for Max. She set the alarm on her phone for fifteen minutes as a reminder to head back when it went off. With Tuck and Silas bundled into the double jogging stroller, Alice took off down the street. Max loped along beside her, randomly stopping to sniff this or that, and then running to catch up with them.

The stroller had been worth every penny. It meant that she could fit in a workout at least a couple times a week when Bill was home, and if the run during piano lessons worked, as it seemed to, there was another. It might be too much trouble to pack the stroller into the car to take to park day, although that was another option. Alice found that getting a run in made her whole day better. It helped her sleep more soundly, and that in turn helped her maintain patience throughout the day. Of course, the prolactin from nursing didn't hurt either. She reached for a swig from her water bottle just as the alarm on her phone sounded.

"What was that, Mommy?" Tuck craned his neck to look up at her.

"Just my alarm, telling me it's time for us to turn around!" she said, making a wide U-turn with the stroller and reaching over to tickle Tuck's sticky chin. She noted their shadow, short, as it was close to noon on this late June day. Then she picked up the pace, in order to make it back in time for Isaac's lesson.

Alice arrived back at the house, sweaty and breathing hard, just as Willy was finishing up. A quick shower with the babies, and then she'd start the lasagne for tonight's potluck.

WITH Silas strapped into his high chair, Alice put water on to boil, and skimmed the recipe to see how to divvy up jobs. Willy got to work chopping onions and garlic while Lucy skinned the carrots. Tuck fooled around with the cheese grater before losing interest and turning to the pots and pans cabinet. As long as he didn't make enough noise to disturb Isaac's lesson, that was OK. Having passed the carrots to Willy for chopping, Lucy turned to the abandoned cheese grater. When Willy finished chopping, he announced that he would be in charge of sautéing the meat and vegetables.

"Can I have a turn?" Lucy looked up from her pile of cheese.

"How about this? Willy sautés the meat and veggies, and you make the spice mixture and mix that into the sauce?"

"OK!" Alice got a tablespoon and a teaspoon, and set them down near Lucy along with the spices and a small bowl.

"Let's see. The recipe calls for two teaspoons of oregano, and two tablespoons of basil." A conversation ensued about which measuring spoon was bigger and by how much. Taking her job very seriously, Lucy carefully measured the spices, opting to use only the teaspoon in lieu of the tablespoon, and counting out loud as she scooped and tipped the seasonings into the small bowl.

When the veggies and meat were browned, Lucy climbed up on the step stool, poured the tomatoes and spices into the pan, and stirred.

Alice could hear Kevin and Isaac finishing up in the other room. Perfect timing. They could all have lunch while the sauce simmered, and then finish the lasagne assembly after.

Wiping her hands on a dishtowel, she went into the family room.

"Kevin, do you want to stay for lunch?"

"Thanks! But I can't. I've got more lessons to get to. Are you guys going to Teresa and Russell's tonight?"

"Yes! We're just now making lasagne to bring."

"I can smell it." He inhaled deeply and rubbed circles over his stomach. "I'll see you guys there."

Lucy, listening from the kitchen, ran out and jumped up and down excitedly in front of Kevin. "Hurray!"

Kevin mussed her hair as much as was possible given the various ponytails.

Isaac straightened the music on the piano and got up from the bench. He held up his hand to say bye to Kevin. "Cool. See you later."

"Yeah. Isaac, do you want me to bring my guitar tonight and show you a few chords?"

Isaac's response was an enthusiastic, "Yes!"

After lunch, Alice set up the pan to begin the lasagne assembly line.

Isaac reminded her that he was going to his job helping Mrs. Renfrew in her garden that afternoon. He was planning to walk the mile by himself. The first time he had done it, he had made a wrong turn and ended up walking for a good ten minutes before realizing it. It had made him twenty minutes late and he hadn't thought to call Mrs. Renfrew.

"All right. Remember your phone and text me when you get there."

"Yup." The back door slammed behind him.

ISAAC liked the crunching sound his shoes made on the gravel by the side of the road. Now that he had the new smart phone, he figured he could use the map if he needed to, but he was pretty sure he knew the way. He wouldn't make the same mistake twice.

Mrs. Renfrew was pretty cool. Sometimes she worked beside him in the garden, and sometimes she showed him what needed to be done and trusted him to do it himself. She'd poke her head out the door once in a while, or bring him a cold drink and they'd get chatting. Last week she showed him the sweater she was knitting, and offered to teach him how to knit if he was interested. She thought starting with a scarf would be a good idea. Mrs. Renfrew could even knit in the dark, which she'd learned to do during World War II during blackouts. She had lots of stories about the Depression and World War II, and Isaac had a willing ear. Mom thought that an interview with Mrs. Renfrew might make a good article for the newspaper, *Acorn,* he published with some of his friends. Starting the newspaper had been Zoe's idea. She wanted it to be a "literary magazine," but so far Isaac had been submitting interviews or research articles instead of writing stories or poems, and it seemed to be enough to keep him on the editorial board, which was the fun part. For the last issue he'd interviewed Kevin. He'd have to come up with something fast for the next issue, or Zoe would start bugging him.

BACK at the ranch, the assembly line was in full swing. With Silas safely in the backpack, Alice put down a layer of noodles, Willy ladled sauce over them, Lucy dolloped and sprinkled cheese, Tuck got a piece of noodle dipped in sauce placed in his baby-bird-wide-open mouth, and so on until the casserole was full and placed in the oven.

After lunch, stories in bed usually worked to lull Tuck into a nap. Once he was asleep, Alice crept out and, switching on the baby monitor, plopped on the couch to nurse Silas. Willy was sitting on the floor amid an assortment of Legos. He had recently gotten a motor and was trying to figure out how to animate one of his creations. Lucy, feet folded beneath her, raked through the cubes and started sorting them by color.

"Do you guys want me to read aloud? Or Lucy, do you want me to get your shells down while Tuck's asleep and we can look through them with the field guide?"

Lucy shot upright. "Can we, can we, can we?!"

Alice transferred Silas to his sister's lap and pulled down the special box from a high shelf. She maneuvered Silas into his sling and headed with Lucy into the kitchen where there was room on the table to lay out the shells. Lucy lifted the lid off and examined the contents. Some shells were tucked carefully with cotton balls in smaller boxes. There was a jar about a third full of just jingles. Alice put some music on softly and fetched the field guide, some labels, and a pen. She and Lucy would sort through and see what shells they could identify and then Lucy would make labels for them. Alice suspected that her shell collection would be what Lucy would want to share at the Science Fair next fall if Teresa organized it again.

"Mommy. Can we go to Florida so I can find a junonia?"

"Maybe someday."

"When are we going to Cape Cod?"

"We have the HoLT camping trip at the end of the summer."

"OK. I need to find more jingles."

Willy looked up from his creation. The sound of the school bus roaring away from the stop outside had disturbed his thought process.

"I think I hear Tommy."

"Mm hmm."

"Mom, I'm going out."

"OK."

"Me too!" Lucy jumped down from the table.

"OK you guys. You can go out but you've got to clean up these little pieces before Tuck gets up from his nap."

"Mommy will you help me?" asked Lucy.

"Yup." Alice and Lucy carefully packed the shells up again. Willy set his car-in-the-making on a high shelf and made a show of scooping the rest of the Legos into the box, put the cover on and shoved it in the corner.

As Alice returned the shells to their safe spot, she saw Willy, Lucy, and Max run by the window outside. In the family room, she squatted to pick up the rest of the Lego pieces and returned them to the box. She grabbed the baby monitor and her phone, and went to sit out on the porch steps. Her phone lit up with a text from Isaac. Not only had he made it to Mrs. Renfrew's, he was on his way home. Oh well. It was progress.

She lifted Silas out of the sling and took his diaper off, then sat him in the grass. Like all her babies, Silas loved a little naked time. She watched him weeble wobble over and then figure out how to get back up. She saw Lucy in her helmet, wheeling her bike down the driveway. Willy would likely spend the rest of the afternoon playing pickup basketball with the neighbors at the end of the street.

"Look who I found!" yelled Isaac as he rounded the corner to their street followed by Max. Seeing his pack out and about, Max bounded up tail wagging, nuzzling Silas and causing him to topple over again, slobbering Alice, and then heading off to see what Willy was up to. Alice had forgotten that Max had gone out with the kids.

"Where was he?"

"I caught him in the act over in the Mahoney's yard."

At least he hadn't wandered far. The baby monitor was making rustling noises.

"Isaac, any chance you cleaned it up?"

"No, Mom. I didn't have a bag."

"Can you do it now?"

"Sure. If I can find it."

Alice gathered Silas up and went in to greet Tuck, who was rubbing sleep from his eyes. She'd better get a snack into him before he asked to nurse, or before Lucy offered him a mud pie for high tea.

Isaac returned successful and chucked the poop bag into the trash barrel, washed his hands, and then joined Tuck for a snack at the kitchen table. "What are you reading in book group now?" Alice asked Isaac. She didn't worry about spoiling a twelve-year-old's appetite even though they would be leaving for the potluck in less than an hour.

"We're going to read aloud *A Midsummer Night's Dream,* but first watch the movie, and choose parts."

"That sounds fun. Does that mean you don't have any reading this week?"

"Well, we're supposed to read a version of the play so we're familiar with the characters. I don't think it will take me that long, though."

The sound of Lucy sobbing turned their heads to the door.

"She fell off her bike," said Willy as he deposited Lucy on the kitchen floor and raced back outside.

"Uh oh! Come on Nurse Tuck. Let's go make Lucy feel all better." Tuck had climbed down from his chair and was patting Lucy's cheek. Alice handed Silas off to Isaac and headed to the bathroom with Lucy and Tuck.

"Bummer! Looks like your leggings tore. But good thing you had something covering your knee or it might have been worse, right?" Lucy's sobs had quieted and she blinked back tears and nodded solemnly. Alice reached down the antibiotic and the Band-Aids. She handed one to Tuck.

"Nurse Tuck, can you please ready a bandage for the patient?"

Lucy smiled through her tears. Alice helped her get the leggings off, trying to avoid further pain to the poor cut knee. She cleaned it and then dabbed it with antibiotic. Ready for the Band-Aid, she turned to Tuck, who was fiercely gripping the one she'd given him.

"Tuck has a boomby."

Alice and Lucy exchanged knowing looks, and Lucy got down from the toilet to help Tuck put the Band-Aid on his perfectly fine knee. Then Nurse Tuck helped Alice bandage Lucy's knee.

"OK sweetie," said Alice, taking Lucy's face in her hands and smooching each of her tear stained cheeks. "Go find a new outfit to put on. It's time to head over to Reesie's."

Isaac had settled in front of the computer, bouncing Silas on his lap. In the kitchen, Alice took the lasagne out and cut a piece to save for Bill to have tomorrow. It was even better the next day, and she smiled imagining his reaction when he found out he'd get seconds. Then she let Tuck scoop Max's kibble into the dog bowl, swooped the toddler onto her hip and went to the door, ringing the cowbell she used to signal to her brood that it was time to come in. She yelled as loud as she could, "Max! Dinner! William the Third! Time to go!"

CHAPTER 13

Teresa

Thursday, June 20

TERESA stood, hands on hips, surveying the dining room. Vera's "wildflower" bouquet, made up of pretty weeds from the front garden, presided over the table, which was piled with paper plates and napkins. Using the real thing for this crowd would require a level of organization even Teresa wasn't capable of. The well-worn tablecloth added splashes of blue, orange, and pink. Otto had pushed the table against the wall, allowing more space in the center of the room for mingling, and the chairs were set out around the edges of the room. Now Otto was in the backyard, building a fire.

The cups and bottles of seltzer, and a lone bottle of red wine, were in the pantry, and she would ask anyone bringing a dessert to set it in the kitchen, along with the fruit salad she had tossed together. She wanted to have a gluten-free alternative for the new family she hoped would come tonight, and she knew Jewel preferred her kids to avoid sugary desserts, of which there'd be plenty. Vera had made carrot cake cupcakes, and was now working on a welcome sign for the door. Russell would be home in a few minutes.

Teresa uncorked the wine and poured a few sips. She'd spent most of the day getting ready for the potluck, and she needed to decompress before the hordes arrived. She knew no one would care about clutter or confusion, but it gave her pleasure to prepare for her friends. Of course, she'd never forget Alice's "compliment" that she loved coming over because the relaxed state of Teresa's house made Alice feel less pressure about keeping her own place neat.

Alice meant well, but she was pretty much in her own head a lot of the time. The phone call last night had, luckily, gone smoothly. Teresa hadn't been looking forward to talking to Alice about Max, but after reading the email thread that Stacy had started, she realized that unless she spoke to her about it, Alice was likely to bring Max along tonight to the potluck. So she'd dialed Alice.

After several rings, a small voice piped, "Hello!"

"Hi Lucy! It's Reesie. Is your mommy available?"

"I think so."

"May I speak to her please?"

Teresa was accosted by the twin sounds of the phone clattering to the floor and Lucy yelling, "MOMMY! Reesie's calling!"

After a half minute and some more indistinct noises, Teresa heard the sound of the receiver fumbling to the spot between Alice's shoulder and bent head. Then, "Hi Teresa. What's up?"

"Well, tomorrow's the potluck."

"I know! We're all looking forward to it."

"Yeah that's part of why I'm calling. As one dog person to another, I realized that you were probably planning on having Max tag along."

"Oh—I guess so."

"Yeah—I don't think it's going to work out. Romeo is going to be super excited, and a lot of people have RSVPed. I don't think it will be a good mix to have Max underfoot as well. Normally I'd suggest him hanging in the backyard, but we're planning to be in and out, so that won't work either. Can he survive a night home alone?"

"Oh sure. I guess I just feel guilty about giving him the amount of attention he needs."

"I know, like a sixth child. Listen, I get it, but I think having him off leash at the park is causing some tension. The kids and I are happy to help walk him and keep an eye on him if you have your hands full with the babies. Or of course I'll always take a baby, you know that."

"Oh thanks, Teresa. I'll take you up on that help. I feel bad about what happened at the park this morning."

"Hey we're all human. See you tomorrow?"

"Yup. Thanks."

WHEN Otto was an infant Teresa had gone to breastfeeding support meetings, and by the time Vera was born she was leading them. That's where she'd met Alice, over a decade ago now, when Alice was getting started nursing Isaac. It was there that Teresa had met the women who accepted as normal and natural her decision to want to be with her kids, and didn't judge her for it. Home-schooling came as a natural extension of that.

She had taken maternity leave suspecting that she didn't want to go back to work as a social worker at the shelter. After Otto was born she went over the household budget with a fine toothed comb to figure out how to make ends meet while giving up her job. She was sure that it was the right choice for her. She had always thought becoming a mother would open a new part of herself that she hadn't yet known about. Once Otto was in her arms nothing could compete with her desire to be with him. She knew she was lucky that Russell's salary could cover them if they cut corners and lived more frugally, and she was grateful to have the option.

What she didn't expect was feeling that she was actually going against the grain to make this choice. She had thought having choices was part of female empowerment, but apparently according to a lot of people, one of the choices had to be employment outside the home. Her own mother, who hadn't had a choice but to stay home with Teresa, thought she was making a big mistake and urged her to go back to work. Little did Teresa know this decision would be the first in a line of decisions that people, even strangers, felt free to pass judgment on. Giving up her job, nursing into toddlerhood, and then, to beat it all, homeschooling!

She didn't remember having had a master plan for her life, other than always wanting to have children. Reflecting now, she had no regrets about taking the path her gut level choices had led her down. Fitting into the culture at large had turned out to be not so important to Teresa. She had continued as a breastfeeding counselor, and now that Vera was eleven, she was thinking of dipping a toe into becoming a postpartum doula.

Homeschooling had been great for the kids, allowing them to pursue interests, play for hours on end, sleep late, have plenty of family time, and avoid arbitrary testing, amongst other things. But it had been equally amazing for her. It's not like she stayed home and closeted herself with her kids. She had the freedom to arrange her life to please her, rather than school's schedule. She had time to pursue her own interests, to put family first, and to make long lasting friendships in this weird little boat of local homeschoolers, riding the waves out here on the fringe. She had learned so much from her kids too, about trusting and respecting children.

Teresa walked into the kitchen and set her wine glass on the table. Romeo click clicked after her and sat sloppily, leaning against the wall. What a doll face. She looked out the back window. Otto was squatting next to the fire pit, stuffing kindling under the logs he had arranged. Years of camping had honed his fire building skills. Every fall, Teresa and Pina organized a camping trip. Everyone in HoLT was invited to reserve a spot in a designated campground. The easy togetherness, the freedom to roam the kids were allowed, the late night singing and talking around the campfire, were all idyllic. What wasn't idyllic were the inevitable issues that arose about in-groups and feeling excluded, and not just with kids, but with the parents! Sometimes she wished she could just go along for the ride like so many people seemed able to do. But in Teresa's experience, you get what you give. Or even really, giving is getting, and putting yourself out there is how you connect, how you make friends. Maybe modern society just teaches people that signing up for something automatically makes you part of it, and consequently they've lost the social skills learned when people need each other.

Her musing was interrupted when Otto hoisted himself off the ground and threw himself, sprawling, into the hammock. What was up with that kid lately? He was maturing into a sometimes moody but overall easy to get along with young man. He had passed out of the awkward stage. He happily helped out with chores now— carrying in groceries, taking the trash out, or moving the laundry along without being asked. He was more independent, eager to get himself places instead of depending on her for a ride. He spent hours in his room doing she wasn't sure what, but then he'd appear and report that he'd written a new guitar tab or computer program.

The idea that she was the "teacher." Ha! Otto had far surpassed her knowledge of computer science and programming. He had the Internet at his disposal, as well as adult friends like Stacy. They could spend hours chatting about all sorts of things that were, frankly, over her head. They had discovered each other on one of Stacy's days off, when she had come along to the park with Sam and the boys. Otto had overheard Stacy telling one of the other parents that she was a programmer, he asked her a question, and they were off. Frisbee game forgotten, they sat in the grass at the edge of the field, deep into algorithms, occasionally using sticks and stones to illustrate a concept. Since then, they usually managed to carve out some time to revisit their common interest whenever their paths crossed, and Otto knew that Stacy was always available if he had a question.

Gazing at Otto out the window, Teresa pondered the dating question. Teresa knew the inner life of a teenage boy was bound to be somewhat overtaken with interest in the topic, but Otto didn't share that with her. He kept that part of his life pretty private, and she wouldn't pry. But she couldn't help wondering what he was thinking. She remembered Nasim's inquisitive glare when he heard they had Cora for the day at the Museum of Science. But that had been her doing, not Otto's. Oh well, she'd probably be the last to know if something were up on that front.

"Mom!" Romeo lurched up from what had become a snooze and ran toward the sound of Vera yelling. Vera skidded into the kitchen with the pug at her heels. "Mom. I finished the sign and I want to make it so when people come, me and Lucy and Emma greet them at the door."

"Sure. Let's see the sign."

Vera pinched its corners and held it up in front of Teresa. "WELCOME HOMESCHOOLERS" was arched by a rainbow, and blue flowers sprouted in the grassy foreground.

"Perfect. That way people should know to just let themselves in if you and your minions want a break."

Vera hunched her shoulders, rubbed her hands together and burped up an evil laugh. Then she straightened up. "Yup! And if we are at the door, hopefully the doorbell won't ring too much and this guy won't have to freak out the whole time." She jumped to the right and then to the left. "Right buddy? You won't get overexcited right?" Romeo dipped into play posture and then took off, tail between legs to run circles around them.

"I guess tiring him out is one strategy. He's definitely on edge today. He knows something's up whenever I start cleaning the house. Will you give the chili a stir?"

Vera gladly tended to the vegetarian chili, which was softly bubbling on the back burner. Classic Vera, to plan on fun with the little girls who were sure to show up, rather than hope for an evening with Sky, only to be disappointed when her good friend cancelled at the last minute. Vera was admirably resourceful. Teresa hoped Jewel would relax at least for today and make it to the potluck at a reasonable hour. Her family needed to eat regardless of how much book work had been accomplished. Teresa shared Pina's sentiment that things might be easier for Jewel and her kids if she could lighten up, but Pina's approach with Jewel was likely to backfire. It just seemed to put Jewel on the defensive. People can only hear what they are ready to hear.

"Mom, I think the chili could use a little more liquid."

Teresa felt that as hostess she didn't have that many options for what to make. She wanted to accommodate the vegans, the gluten-free, the lactose intolerant. Of course the beans in the chili might throw the paleo crowd for a loop, but she just found it hard to believe that a prehistoric human wouldn't eat a bean if they came upon one. Anyway, she'd made a pot of rice, too, and had tortilla chips on hand, as well as tons of optional toppings: shredded cheese, sour cream, guacamole, chopped scallions, so it seemed to her the pickiest person would be able to eat at least something. Hmm, maybe she should have made cornbread, but it was too late now.

"Vera, I trust your judgment. Can you keep an eye on the chili while I take a quick shower?"

"Sure, Mom. Just let me grab my book." Vera returned with *Liar & Spy* and settled herself at the kitchen table.

Teresa hung her towel on a hook and stepped into the shower, letting out a breath. She thought she was ready for the evening ahead. The chili was simmering, the fire built. Oops! The lawn chairs. She'd get Otto to put them out. And ask Vera to set up some candles. Or maybe that was asking for trouble. The furniture in the house had been arranged to accommodate as many people as possible, Vera's sign was at the ready. She'd even vacuumed! A cool breeze let Teresa know that Romeo had pushed the bathroom door open. She poked her head out of the shower and sure enough, he was curled, snoring, on the bathmat. She turned the water off, grabbed her towel, and pulled the curtain aside. Romeo looked up. "Who's so handsome?" she crooned at him.

"You talking to me?" Russell grinned as he peered around the corner into the bathroom, chip and guacamole in hand.

"Oh, good you're home. And don't eat all the guac before people get here."

"Listen, I just want to be sure to get something decent in case it's all chips and salsa."

"I know, I know. Well, I made a big pot of chili, and Pina and Carmen are coming and you know they'll bring good dishes. Listen, I met a woman at the last support meeting, Priscilla, and she might come tonight. Hopefully her husband will come, too. He's not on board for homeschooling, but from what Priscilla said, it sounds like their son could really use a break from school."

"How old is he?"

"The son or the husband?" Russell stretched his eyes open as widely as possible to indicate that she was oh-so-not-funny. "Come on. You know I'm hilarious. The kid's seven."

"OK, I'll keep an eye out."

Teresa didn't set herself up as an "expert" although she knew more about homeschooling than a lot of the self-proclaimed homeschooling gurus. She had just been living this life, talking to interested people, but not trying to sell it. Of course her enthusiasm spilled over when she talked about it with parents considering alternatives. She thanked her instincts for causing her to stumble on a slower way of life that had led to questioning the widely accepted mythology of school.

On her way out of the steamy bathroom, Teresa yelled to Russell.

"Otto built a fire. Can you ask him to help you put out the lawn chairs?"

"Sure, sure," said Russell, grabbing another scoop of guacamole on his way out the back door.

Teresa padded into the bedroom with Romeo at her heels. She put on jeans and a patterned tank top with a little swing to it. She combed her short hair, then bent over and shook it out instead. She paused to consider earrings. Hey, it's a party, why not dress up a little? The silver dangly ones spoke to her. Just then the doorbell rang, Romeo lost it, and Vera flashed by on her way to the front door. It must be six o'clock.

CHAPTER 14

The Potluck

Thursday, June 20

"I GOT it, I got it!" Vera sprinted to the front door with Romeo hot on her heels, sliding along the wood floor of the hallway. He bounced off the shoe crate, then Vera's slim ankle, claws scratching the floorboards. Good thing Russell was in the backyard—he hated the sound. The noise didn't bother Teresa. The fact that she'd neglected Romeo's toenails did.

Pina, Lou, and company had let themselves in and were already spilling into the hallway by the time Vera made it to the door. Darned if Romeo didn't slide right into Dominic, who laughed and crouched down to nuzzle the pug's ears. "Hello!" exclaimed Pina.

"Hi," said Teresa, giving Pina a quick hug and relieving her of the giant casserole she was holding. "Oh, that smells good. Mac and cheese?" Pina nodded. "Well," said Teresa. "Russell is going to be psyched."

Lou hugged Teresa and asked, "Where is the old man?"

"Out back," said Teresa, and Lou promptly turned around to make a beeline for the yard. Vera and Aria remained behind to greet guests, and the rest of them headed for the dining room, where Teresa placed Pina's casserole on the table. "Where's Otto?" asked Anthony.

"Outside making the fire," said Teresa, and Anthony and Dominic were gone in a flash.

Teresa turned toward the kitchen. Pina followed and asked, "Are we expecting a crowd?"

"June potluck, what do you think?" Pina nodded absently, distracted by the food. She lifted the cover off the chili and gave it a good whiff, then turned to inspect the bowls of toppings, sticking her finger into the guacamole. "Stop that," said Teresa. "You're worse than the kids."

"It's so good," she said, licking her finger. "What's in it?"

"I don't know," said Teresa. "Otto made it. Read the ingredient list."

"I don't see it," said Pina as voices sounded in the hallway. She wasn't surprised that Otto had neglected to write down the ingredients. Anthony didn't record what he put in the mac and cheese, either, but since it was Pina's recipe and she knew it by heart, she could make the sign now, if only she could locate a piece of paper.

While Teresa went to the front door to see who'd arrived, Pina looked around and found the chipotle powder on the counter.

"Aha," she said. "Brilliant!"

It was Carmen at the door, of course. Elizabeth and Anne went straight to the backyard while Emma stayed with Vera and Aria, waiting on the doorstep. "Come on," said Teresa, holding the platter of empanadas she'd taken from Lizzie and heading for the dining room.

"Where do you want this?" said Carmen.

"What is it?" asked Teresa.

"Lizzie's chocolate peanut butter pie."

"In the kitchen," said Teresa. "It'll go out later with the desserts."

Carmen entered the kitchen, where she caught Pina sneaking a nibble of shredded cheddar. "Is Lou not here?" she asked, almost hopefully.

Teresa knew that Carmen's question had more to do with Henry's absence than Lou's presence. She glanced at Pina, who was busy scribbling on a piece of paper and hadn't seemed to notice. Pina wasn't the most tactful person in the world. Teresa loved her anyway, and smiled as she recalled an article that she had read just that morning, about blunt friends being the best friends.

"Lou's with Russell," said Teresa, turning to Carmen. "No Henry?"

"Working late," said Carmen. "He'll be here." Teresa and Pina both knew that likely as not, Henry wouldn't show up. Pina finished writing down the mac and cheese ingredients and adopted an about-to-speak-her-truth posture but the commotion at the front door intervened.

"Come on," said Teresa, taking Carmen by the arm and nodding to Pina to follow. "Let's see who's here."

IT WAS Melissa and Gary, with lemon squares made by Zoe. Pina wasn't surprised by that, partly because of the rave reviews they'd gotten when Zoe brought them to book club, and partly because Melissa didn't seem to have energy for anything besides worrying about Jacob.

Pina thought Gary had done the right thing convincing Melissa to pull Jacob from school, but as far as Melissa was concerned, Jacob was floundering. He defied her at every turn, fighting her over the copious amount of schoolwork on which she insisted. Teresa had encouraged Melissa to relax and give Jacob space, but Melissa wasn't sure she could do that. Jacob could read well beyond his age level, Melissa knew that, but his writing was a mess, and how was he supposed to function in life if he couldn't write? Gary was in charge of math, and assured her that Jacob was doing fine, but Melissa needed more than just his word. She wanted to see evidence, why couldn't her husband understand that?

"Hey," said Pina, giving Melissa a hug. "Where have you been hiding?"

"Nowhere," said Melissa. "Just haven't felt like getting out much lately." She wondered what Pina would think if she told her the truth. If there was anyone she could tell, she thought it would be Pina. Most of the parents in the group turned to Teresa, or even Carmen, when they needed emotional support, but there was never any bullshit with Pina, and while her straightforward style made some people uncomfortable, it put Melissa at ease.

"I'm glad you came," said Pina, which made Melissa feel better instantly. Pina wouldn't say it if she didn't mean it.

The sound of Romeo barking and a child crying distracted them. "Uh oh," said Pina. "Somebody doesn't like dogs." She looked outside to see Priscilla, the new woman from the last support meeting, holding a small, crying girl. Beside her stood a man shaking Teresa's hand, and a little boy hiding behind the man's legs.

Pina watched as Teresa scooped up Romeo and tried to calm him while the woman comforted the little girl. To Pina the newbies looked younger every year. Not that she minded their age, but sometimes she took exception to their neediness.

"That kid looks worried," said Melissa, watching the little boy peeking at Tarek, who'd just arrived with his parents.

"He's probably just shy," said Pina.

Teresa gave Nasim and Sarah quick hugs, then went into the house with Romeo. "Just put the food on the dining room table," she said, heading upstairs. Pina knew she was going to try and settle Romeo in one of the kids' rooms, probably with a bone, something which she should have done in the first place. Dog people were something Pina would never understand.

Speaking of which, Alice and her brood were arriving. Pina was relieved to see they didn't have Max in tow. She knew Teresa had talked to Alice about bringing the dog, but Pina wouldn't have put it past Alice to show up with Max, anyway.

Hot on the heels of Alice and her unwieldy pack were Sam and Stacy and their boys. As far as Pina was concerned, there was an example of someone who knew how to deal with an active kid. The younger one, Jasper, got into everything, but observing Sam's patience and acceptance of her child's personality warmed Pina's heart. It reminded her of why she started homeschooling in the first place, back when Anthony was in nursery school and the teachers were already talking about his attention span and hyperactivity.

The way Pina had seen it, Anthony's energy was an asset. She believed squashing it with tedious desk work, stupid behavior charts, or medication would do her child a disservice. Besides, was it his fault he was born in an urban area with little space to roam, and a culture where sitting still was prized? If they lived on a farm he'd run around and explore all day and no one would bat an eye. To the best of her ability, Pina had tried to offer Anthony the equivalent space, and even though he still drove her crazy a lot of the time with his forgetfulness and his struggles to stay organized for his community college classes, he was a vibrant, creative kid who was hugely excited about baseball, chess, cooking, and life in general.

"Let's clear the hallway," said Carmen. The throngs were arriving, and Carmen was relieved to see Bill hadn't come with Alice. At least she wasn't the only one whose partner didn't show—yet, anyway. Carmen tried not to be jealous of other people's marriages but trying never worked. Even though she knew she shouldn't, she often compared herself and her kids to others. No amount of self-talk could stop it. It felt as though the trait was in her genes, some kind of annoying mutation that popped up way too much.

Pina had already disappeared into the dining room, no doubt to check out the food. Carmen shook her head—that woman was obsessed. Sam and family had to fight their way through Alice's clan, which was spread out haphazardly on the front steps, Alice holding Silas while Tuck melted down because Romeo had been sequestered, and Willy stood complaining about something Isaac had done to him. Lucy had joined Vera and Aria and Emma, who all had enough sense to move out of the way when people were trying to get in the house. Carmen couldn't help but notice the annoyed look on Sam's face as they stepped their way around Alice's crisis.

"Hi, Carmen," Sam said when she saw her. Carmen wasn't Sam's favorite "veteran," as Stacy referred to the older moms (that would be Teresa), but she still liked her. She liked all the parents, for the most part, except Alice. No one pushed her buttons the way Alice did.

"Hi," said Carmen, greeting the four of them but feeling distracted by the arrival of Ellen and Cora. She wanted to talk to Ellen but before she knew it Ellen and her daughter had slid right by, saying hello to Teresa, who'd made it back downstairs in time to greet the new arrivals. Oh well, there'd be plenty of time for Carmen to chat Ellen up. Now to go talk to the newbies.

"WHERE'S Jewel?" Sam hoped she'd show up. Jasper really liked Rock and expected to be able to play with him.

"I'm sure she'll be along," said Teresa. "She's always late."

"Reesie, you know she's not coming unless her kids finish their work," said Pina.

Of course Teresa knew that, but what was the point of saying it? Sam had been around long enough to know it, too, and to deal with it firsthand. Jasper had been disappointed more than once by cancelled playdates with Rock. Normally Sam found Pina's frankness refreshing, but this time she didn't like the judgmental tone. As far as Sam was concerned, Jewel was only trying to be a good mom and do what she thought was best for her kids, just like the rest of them.

"Dig in, everyone," Teresa called. "Food's in the dining room, big pot of chili with toppings is in the kitchen." People started to eat, filling up paper plates and bowls. Pina quickly disappeared to get in line, and found herself behind the new dad. "Hi," she said, holding out her hand. "I'm Pina."

"Ron," he said, with a quick handshake that seemed reluctant. "This is Felix."

Felix pointed to the mac and cheese and said, "Can I have that, Dad?"

"Sorry," said Ron. "Looks like gluten." He quickly read the available ingredient lists and said, "You can have this salad, and some hummus, and the chicken we brought." Typically, there weren't many options for his son, but this was better than usual, and at least there were ingredient lists and separate utensils for everything.

"There's chili on the stove," said Pina.

"I want some of that!" said Felix.

"OK, kid," said Ron, turning to Pina. "Excuse us."

Pina thought Ron didn't seem happy about being at the potluck, which fit with what Priscilla had said at the support meeting. Pina wondered whether Ron had even glanced at the reading material she'd suggested Priscilla share with him. She didn't doubt that Priscilla had provided it. Pina hoped she'd have a moment later to talk with Ron. Any help she could give a desperate mom, she'd give.

The line seemed to be moving slowly, and one glance at the table revealed why. Sarah was there, picking up each ingredient list and reading it like it was some kind of dissertation. Sarah really appreciated the lists, but deciphering some people's handwriting wasn't easy, something Pina wouldn't notice since she never read them. Many were obviously penned by kids, and those were generally the easiest to read. The scribbly cursive on Alice's lasagne was another matter, but Sarah waded through it and dished herself up a piece.

She also served herself some mac and cheese and grabbed a few of the beef empanadas, cringing when she saw that the veggie ones were made with canola oil. Nice of Carmen to be so accommodating, but canola oil? She'd have to mention its dangers to her. Sarah finished filling up her plate with some salad, and a little of the hummus and Syrian bread they'd brought. Nasim made excellent hummus, but still, for Sarah it was slightly embarrassing to show up at a potluck with it.

Her embarrassment grew as she watched Pina, then Alice, bypass it. Willy seemed to like it, anyway. He was in the process of dumping almost half the bowl on his plate before Pina stopped him. Alice, as usual, hadn't noticed.

"Hey, Sarah," said Alice, moving away from the dining room table to where Sarah stood munching on an empanada.

"Hi, Alice," she said. Silas was sleeping soundly in the purple sling Sarah had handed down to Alice when Lucy came along. Alice held her plate out in front of it, resting it on the rounded lump of Silas's butt and taking a bite of macaroni.

"Oh, this is so good," she said. "Pina's macaroni is the best."

Sarah nodded. "Love it," she said. "Your lasagne is delicious, too."

Alice smiled. "Thanks. And thanks for taking Willy last weekend." Alice really meant it. Since Silas was born, she'd been having an increasingly hard time dealing with Willy. He wasn't practicing or reading many books, instead choosing to immerse himself in *Minecraft* or play basketball with the neighborhood kids. Those things would be fine if he'd just listen to her when she asked him to do something. Getting chummy with Tarek seemed to help, at least temporarily. He'd been much happier and more responsive when he came home from the sleepover.

"Oh, it was our pleasure," said Sarah. "They had a great time." Tarek was one of the few only children in the pack, and although he seemed to have no trouble socializing in groups, Sarah worried that he spent too much time alone. He loved having Willy over, and Sarah had gotten to spend quality time with the two of them, making banana cookies and playing *Jenga* and *Masterpiece*.

"Hey," she said. "I've been meaning to ask you if Willy's free next weekend," she said. "I'd love to take them to the museum."

"Sure," said Alice. "What museum?"

"The art museum."

"Really?" Alice was surprised, and not sure how well that would go over with her second son.

"Yes," said Sarah. "We played *Masterpiece* and Willy loved the postcards of the paintings. I mentioned the museum and he seemed excited."

"Oh," said Alice. "OK." The conversation caused her a twinge of guilt—fine art was something she hadn't exposed her kids to much, if at all, and here Willy seemed to be interested in it. The guilt passed quickly, though, as Silas stirred in his sling and Carmen showed up with Tuck in her arms.

"His face was covered with lemon bar and he was about to crucify Lizzie's pie when I found him," she said.

Alice thought Carmen seemed annoyed, which annoyed her. How did Carmen expect a two-year-old to behave? Fortunately, Tuck wasn't crying. Quite the contrary, he was busily licking his sticky fingers. Alice looked around for a place to put down her plate so she could attend to Tuck.

"Let me," said Sarah, taking Tuck from Carmen. "Alice, find yourself a seat and finish eating."

A wave of gratitude flooded Alice. "Thank you so much," she said, slipping away quickly before Carmen could say another word.

THE spread was glorious. Nasim didn't have nearly enough room in his stomach to eat as much as he wanted of the food he stood surveying, but he loved looking at it. The overflowing table reminded him of family gatherings when he was a kid, his mother's Sheikh Mahshi, his grandmother's jasmine rice with crispy crust, the lemony stuffed grape leaves that were his father's specialty, and the gaymar his cousins always made, served with fresh bread and date syrup.

He had no regrets about the decision he and Sarah had made to have only one child, but he'd grown up in a big family, and sometimes he missed it. Luckily, the community they'd found through homeschooling made up for it a lot of the time.

Nasim had intentionally made himself last in line, so he could take his time and enjoy looking at the food. There was Pina's famous casserole, rich with gooey cheese and glistening sausage, more than half gone now.

Alice's lasagne also had a big dent in it, but it had been so well constructed it still held its shape. Nasim observed its many layers, first the saucy red foundation and the curly noodles laid upon it, then chunky smatterings of ground meat and different kinds of cheese, creamy ricotta and smushy mozzarella and heaps of parmesan, followed by more red sauce, more curly noodles, more of everything. He carefully carved a rectangle, placed it on his plate, and moved on.

Next were Carmen's empanadas, also famous in HoLT circles, their half-moon shapes looking like smiles, their perfectly crimped edges crispy and brown. The beef were going fast, but there were enough for Nasim to take two. He even grabbed one from the veggie platter, which was still loaded.

He also helped himself to plenty of the warm green bean salad brought by Stacy and Sam. As he dished it up he appreciated the inclusion of lightly toasted pine nuts, and the heady, garlicky aroma.

Lucky for him to be last, because it allowed him to be the first to partake of the green salad that had just arrived with Jewel's big brood. It was full of big chunks of leaf lettuce, rounds of purple carrots, shredded red cabbage, salty sunflower seeds, and the season's first strawberries. Nasim waited patiently while Sky dressed it with oil and balsamic vinegar, chatting with her about the Maya exhibit he'd recently visited at the museum. Normally she'd talk with him enthusiastically, but now she wanted to get outside and be with her friends, so she didn't have much to say and left in a hurry after a perfunctory toss of the salad. Nasim smiled, understanding.

There was just enough room on his plate for the Syrian bread and hummus he'd brought, and though he knew Sarah disapproved of their contribution, he couldn't disagree more. He had perfected his recipe when he was in college, smooth and creamy with plenty of lemon and garlic, chick peas, and a sheen of olive oil spread over the top like liquid gold.

Teresa's chili was on the stove, a giant pot of spicy, tomato-y goodness that would be his second course. For now, he'd take his time and appreciate every bite of these offerings, and the dear friends who brought them.

THE backyard was full of people. Joy and Rock came running, which meant Jewel had arrived. Dominic and Anne called to them. "Where's Sky?"

They ignored the question. Joy headed for the huddle of Tyler, Lucy, Tarek, and Willy, who were examining a snail. Joy jumped in to help Lucy and Tyler fashion a bed of moss for it while Willy and Tarek brainstormed ways to repair its cracked shell. Rock ran straight for Jacob and Jasper, who were practicing karate katas next to the garage.

Dominic was about to suggest to Anne that they go find Sky when she came bounding into the backyard herself. Dominic asked, "What took you so long?"

"I had to dress the salad," said Sky.

"No, I mean why are you so late?"

Sky grimaced and said, "Rock, as usual."

Over in the hammock, Zoe and Elizabeth and Cora snuggled while Zoe good naturedly reprimanded Elizabeth for missing the *Acorn* deadline. "Sorry," she said. "We were supposed to see the movie last weekend but my orchestra conductor called an extra rehearsal."

"Are you telling me you haven't even seen the movie?" Zoe said. Elizabeth shrugged and nodded.

"Can't you write about something else?"

Cora, seeing an opportunity to please Zoe, said, "I just finished *A Drowned Maiden's Hair*. I can write a review."

Zoe hadn't heard of the book, but Cora had good taste, and she needed content. "Can you get it to me tomorrow?"

"Of course," said Cora, even though tomorrow was her first day volunteering to shelf read at the library, which meant she'd be up way too late writing.

"Look," said Elizabeth. "It's Kevin."

"Oh, awesome!" said Zoe. Kevin came to her house every week to teach Jacob piano, and always hung around after to talk. Sometimes her mom was there, too, which was great, since Kevin had homeschooled his whole life and her mom seemed to need a lot of reminders that it was a good thing to do.

"You brought it!" said Isaac when he saw what Kevin was holding.

"Yup," said Kevin, patting his guitar case.

"Take it out!" said Isaac.

Kevin laughed. "How about you take it out so I can get something to eat?" Isaac positioned himself on a lawn chair and gingerly lifted the guitar from its case while Kevin went to find dinner.

On his way, he nodded to Priscilla and Felix, hanging onto his mother's leg for dear life, and passed Otto, Anthony, Vera, and Aria, busily perfecting the bonfire.

Priscilla watched them. At first, she'd been horrified that kids had been left to work on the fire without adult help, but she forced her preconceptions aside (she needed to believe in this, she really did) and simply observed. It wasn't long before she found herself impressed with their abilities. More and more, she liked what she saw. She hoped Ron would, too. He'd been inside for a while without her. Maybe that meant he was meeting people and getting convinced. Felix pulling on her skirt distracted her. "Mommy," he said.

He tried to drag her to the corner of the yard where Isaac sat playing with the guitar—playing with, Priscilla thought, because he obviously wasn't making music. She glanced around, trying to find someone who looked closer to Felix's age. Gabby, no surprise, had found a playmate right away, and was off making fairy houses with a little girl named Emma. She wasn't the one who needed to fit in with this bunch, though. "Honey," said Priscilla, pointing to Jasper and Rock, "let's go over there."

"No, Mommy." Felix kept dragging her and finally she relented, knowing that if she tried to force him he'd have a tantrum. By the time they reached Isaac, Kevin had returned with a full plate.

"Welcome back," Isaac said. "How's the food?"

"Your mom's lasagne is always good," said Kevin. "Hi," he said, turning to Priscilla and Felix. "I'm Kevin."

Priscilla was about to introduce herself when Felix started fidgeting and saying loudly, "Can I play? Can I play?" She felt the familiar embarrassment rise up in her. When she picked Felix up from school and he behaved this way, the teachers immediately chastised him for his volume and inappropriate behavior. She thought about intervening, but she couldn't get on her knees, take him by the shoulders, look him in the eye, and firmly tell him to stop the way the teachers did. It just didn't feel right to her, and besides, it rarely worked.

"Sure," said Kevin, smiling. "Can you wait a minute? I need to show Isaac a couple things first."

"OK," said Felix, sitting cross-legged on the grass.

"What's your name?" asked Kevin.

"Felix."

Kevin turned to Priscilla, holding out his hand. She shook it and said, "Priscilla."

"Nice to meet you," said Kevin, kneeling beside Isaac. "That looks good," he said. "You know how to hold it, and that's a pretty good strum." Isaac smiled widely. "Let's start with E minor," said Kevin, and proceeded to show Isaac the fingering.

When Isaac successfully played a real chord Kevin commended his work, and Felix laughed out loud and clapped. He'd been riveted the whole time, which astonished Priscilla. She really wanted him to make a friend or two tonight, but maybe this was just fine.

"Your turn," said Kevin, looking at Felix. He jumped up and sat in the lawn chair as Isaac slid out. Before they could get to work, Russell came outside and yelled for everyone to come in for a toast.

Priscilla looked at Felix, worried about what his reaction might be. "A toast!" Kevin was saying. "That sounds fun. Let's go check that out. After, I'll teach you a chord, too."

"OK!" said Felix, jumping up and following the crowd into the house. Kevin held Felix's hand when he offered it, and for the first time in a long time, Priscilla felt herself relax about her son. She recognized this was just a moment, but it was one she'd gladly take.

She did, following the rest of what just might become her tribe, past the bonfire, through the warm June air, into the house filled with people.

❖

TERESA'S kitchen wasn't small, but squeezing into it proved challenging. Chuck thought that was all part of the fun. He was squished between Nasim who was holding Blue, and Sarah who was holding Tuck, and they were all playing a raucous game of peek-a-boo with the little boys. If you asked Chuck, there wasn't anything in the world—anything—like the belly laughs of babies, even if they were big babies.

As everyone piled in from outdoors, the big kids awkwardly worked their way into the crowd. Chuck looked across the room at Jewel, who'd been having a meaningful conversation with Sam before the adolescents started stomping in. Anthony stepped on her toe and she shrieked in spite of herself. "Ouch!"

Anthony immediately apologized, looking so sheepish Jewel couldn't very well hang onto her annoyance. As Chuck watched all this, he could almost hear his wife's inner dialogue. All that yoga and she still couldn't manage to be less uptight. He knew it came from love, and her drive to give the kids a better childhood than she'd had, but as much as Jewel craved perfection, it simply wasn't an option, especially with teenagers who couldn't even read their own space half the time. He remembered well how clumsy he'd been at that age.

Russell quieted the din with a whistle, high and bright. The room felt steamy, the heat exacerbated by the gently simmering chili on the stove and the presence of so many bodies huddled together. Chuck lifted his glass of wine and took a big swallow, and Jewel gave him an admonishing look. He knew he was supposed to wait for the toast but he had plenty in his glass, he'd just refilled it, and it was good red wine—Russell and Teresa always had good wine.

Chuck winked at Jewel and she smiled. He was the most happy-go-lucky person she'd ever met, and despite the fact that she complained about his lack of organization half the time, his joie de vivre pleased her.

"Welcome, everyone, to the annual June potluck bash!" Russell loved to make pronouncements, especially in his own home. "This is an important year," he said.

Teresa, standing in the corner with Pina and Henry (he'd arrived only forty five minutes late, much to Carmen's relief), listened to her husband, wondering what he was going to say. She hoped it wouldn't be anything too syrupy. Last year he'd gone on a little too long (in reality it was just a few seconds) about her contributions to the community. Pina and Carmen had been mentioned, too, but they didn't seem to mind the attention. "This year for the first time," Russell continued, "bonfire duties have been fully passed to the next generation."

What a relief, he was focusing on the kids. As the crowd began to cheer, Teresa looked at Otto and saw his cheeks were flushing pink. Was it the heat or embarrassment? He really was too much like her. Anthony stood next to him, victory fists raised, head nodding. Vera and Aria raised their fists, too, and laughed.

"Before the sun goes down and we head outside, I want to acknowledge the effort we all put into making this group work." More cheers. "Especially, of course, my beautiful wife Reesie." Louder cheers, Teresa turning red, Pina nudging her, Carmen smiling.

"I'd also like to thank all the cooks, especially the dessert cooks. That means you, Vera and Zoe and Lizzie and Cora."

Vera blew her dad a kiss. Elizabeth gave a small smile. Zoe nodded and screwed her face into an aw-it-was-nothing kind of look while Cora beamed, as much at Zoe as at Russell's compliment. Ellen looked at the four of them and thought she couldn't remember when her daughter looked so happy.

Russell peeked at the piece of paper Teresa had stuffed into his palm and continued. "We also have Priscilla and Ron, and their kids Felix and Gabby, attending their first HoLT potluck." Priscilla waved to the people gathered in the room as Teresa came up beside her and put a hand on her shoulder. It was a small gesture, so the emotional weight it seemed to convey surprised Priscilla, or maybe it was the sight of her husband. He was standing next to Carmen and smiling, and it didn't even look forced.

"So," continued Russell. "Let's raise our glasses and drink to HoLT, and another great year together!" Cheers erupted again, and wine, seltzer, ginger ale, and apple juice were imbibed.

Before the crowd had a chance to disperse, Rock made his way through his father's legs into the edge of the circle of people. "Hey, buddy," said Chuck, lifting his son, whose cheeks were smeared with sticky goo.

"What is all over his face?" called Jewel from across the room. She'd seen the creamy smudges immediately.

Sarah turned around to look at the dessert table behind them and saw a big chunk scooped out of the chocolate peanut butter pie, likely with a hand—Rock's hand. "It's just pie," she said.

People were reforming into conversational groups as Jewel made her way across the room. She took her son from Chuck, too angrily, it occurred to her as he covered his face with his hands. "Rock," she cried. "That was wrong!" She turned to Chuck and said, "He's already too hyper, he can't eat all that sugar!"

Rock's arms were reaching toward Chuck, his body squirming wildly. Chuck took him back and Rock buried his face in his father's shoulder. "It's fine," said Chuck. "A little sugar never hurt anybody."

"And what about poor Lizzie," said Jewel. "All the work she put into making it." Rock never looked up, but Jewel hoped he was listening.

Elizabeth came by with her dessert plate full of fruit, a cupcake, one of Cora's fudgy tarts, and a sliver of her pie. "It's OK, Rock," she said, putting a hand on his back. "I made it so people could eat it." Rock turned slightly so one smiling eye looked at Elizabeth. "Was it good?" she asked, in a tone that said she knew very well it was delicious.

Rock lifted his head quickly, like a jack-in-the-box. "Oh, yeah!" he said.

"Jewel," Pina began, and Jewel cringed inside. Where did *she* come from, and why did she always have to be around at moments like this? "You know what they say about forbidden fruit."

Sam had shown up, too, Jewel gratefully noted. Sam wanted to come up with something pithy to say in response to Pina, but she couldn't think of anything. Maybe someday she'd have the nerve to confront Pina, but not today. She could still try and help her friend. "Hey," she said. "Let's go sit in the living room, Jewel."

On their way they passed Carmen, who'd finally corralled Ellen into a conversation. So far, it had been the usual, Carmen complimenting Cora's tarts and asking if she could get the recipe. Ellen knew the small talk was just a pretense, and that any moment Carmen would start asking probing questions. "Sure," she said. "I can text it to you right now, what's your number?"

"My phone number?"

"Yes, so I can text you the recipe."

Carmen pointed to the hand-held device Ellen had just pulled from her pocket and said, "You mean one of those? I don't have one of those."

Ellen had been around these homeschoolers long enough not to be shocked by their sometimes inexplicable ways. She didn't know how anyone could live in the twenty-first century without a smart phone, but of course Carmen didn't have a job or many responsibilities that Ellen could see, and while *she* could never tolerate that, she supposed it could make life simpler. "It's just on a friend's cooking blog. I'll have Cora send Elizabeth the link, how's that?"

"Sure," said Carmen, obviously about to speak again. Ellen peered into the living room and could see Sam and Jewel sitting on the couch. She would have liked nothing better than to join them, but before she could make excuses to do so, Carmen said, "I'm sorry if I upset you by mentioning your husband."

"Oh," said Ellen. It wasn't a very articulate response, but that's what happened whenever someone mentioned James. "It's OK," she said. "I don't mind." Why did she say that? She did mind.

Carmen looked relieved. "Is Cora coming to Elizabeth's birthday party next week?" Ellen hadn't really thought about it, and with the big job she was starting, she didn't feel like she could make any promises. "Gary's bringing Zoe, and your place is on the way. I mentioned it to him and he said he'd be happy to pick up Cora."

"Wow," said Ellen. "Thank you. I know she'd love it. I'll check with Gary right now." Carmen herself had given Ellen the excuse to leave the conversation, and although she took it, she left thinking she might have judged Carmen too harshly. She'd always had an edge, or so she'd been told. It had been James that softened it, but with him gone, and the grief, and Cora's foundering, she'd grown it back. With Cora thriving, maybe she could let it go again.

TERESA had let Romeo back downstairs and he was visiting everyone in the living room, including Tarek and Willy and Aria building block structures in the corner, and Jewel and Sam eating fruit salad on the couch, recently joined by Stacy, who held a steaming cup of coffee. All parties had to protect their treasures from the pug, the kids forming a wall to keep him from knocking down their building, inside of which currently dwelled Tarek's amazing Lego dinosaur, and the women raising their plates and cup high in the air.

"Come on, boy," said Vera, intending to take the dog into the backyard.

Alice stood on the outskirts of the room. She'd had a nice conversation with Sarah, and chatted a little with Gary and the new dad, Ron, but it had been a long day and she really wanted a comfortable seat before they all hung out around the bonfire later. Fortunately, the seat next to Sam was open.

"Hi," she said, taking it.

Stacy and Jewel both greeted her, and so did Sam, although she didn't smile. She rarely did when Alice was around. Alice didn't take it personally. Seeing Romeo made her remember about Max, and she hoped he wasn't too lonely by himself in the house. "Oh, I hope Max is OK," she said, thinking out loud.

"Thanks for leaving him at home," said Stacy, and for a split second Alice thought she might actually leave it at that. Then she added, "He really should be leashed at the park."

Alice felt awkward. She didn't know Stacy well, and she wasn't sure she wanted to. "Yeah," she agreed. "Of course."

Sam was sorting through a host of feelings, including simultaneous annoyance and admiration at Stacy's social straightforwardness. "Where's Tyler?" Stacy asked Sam.

"Last time I saw him he was out back," she answered, "belting 'Let It Go' with Lucy."

Alice looked at Tarek and Aria and Willy building some kind of fortress around Tarek's Lego dinosaur. The sight made her remember what had happened at Presentation Night. If Tuck were there right now, he'd be joining right in on the building, wanting to play with the big kids. Given Stacy's presence and her obvious opinions, Alice felt glad that Tuck was elsewhere. Really, she didn't know what people like Stacy, and even Carmen, thought she was supposed to do. Forbid her toddler from exploring and playing? Punish him for something he didn't even understand? What good would come of that? None of them had as many kids as she did. The only one who went through similar problems was Jewel (look what just happened with Rock and the pie). Alice would have liked to become better friends with her, but it seemed that every time she'd tried to get their kids together, Jewel would cancel for some reason.

Right now, Jewel looked to be having a fine time with Sam. They were talking about yoga, something Alice cared little about. She looked out the window, at the clusters of laughing, playing people, and the now robust flames. Time to go find Bill and Tuck and snuggle around the fire.

"OH MY god," said Cora. "I'm so sorry, Zoe."

"It's OK," said Zoe. "Hopefully it won't actually happen."

Cora hugged her, maybe a little too hard, but still it felt nice. Zoe had been pretty upset when she arrived at the potluck, although no one would have known it. That's what she thought, anyway, but apparently Cora had noticed. She'd been waiting all night to get Zoe alone, and once it was finally just the two of them in the hammock, she was able to turn to Zoe and ask if she was OK. Zoe replied in the affirmative, but still went ahead and told Cora about the fights her parents had been having, and how as she was quietly arranging the lemon squares on their best platter, she overheard her dad telling her mom he thought they should separate.

Zoe didn't want her parents to split up. Ever since they'd arrived at the potluck her insides had felt like they were all knotted up. The only thing that helped was seeing her mom spending time with Pina. Zoe hoped she was spilling the beans. Pina was no nonsense, which was just the kind of advice her mom needed.

Another hopeful thing had happened, one that made it seem like her mom *had* opened up to Pina. A few minutes before, when everyone was singing rounds around the bonfire, Pina had guided Melissa straight to the spot next to Gary. Zoe felt immensely relieved when she saw her dad take her mom's hand. She hoped it meant he was changing his mind.

"Hey, you two." Elizabeth was back, with Otto and Anthony. "Move over." Cora and Zoe squeezed in tighter to make room for all of them, and Zoe was glad that Otto had taken the spot next to her. With him on one side and Cora on the other, she felt warm and cozy and happy.

Otto had loved the lemon squares, which was good, although she hadn't managed to corral him into showing her the *Acorn* layout—he was too busy talking programming with Stacy. At least there hadn't been any weirdness with Elizabeth.

Zoe turned to Otto, intending to ask when they could make a time to look at *Acorn*, but Elizabeth and Anthony distracted her. "Come on," Anthony said, pulling Elizabeth out of the hammock. "Let's see if there's any pie left."

Everyone else had gone inside. Cora tilted her head to the side and rested it on Zoe's shoulder. Zoe adjusted her body and relaxed further into the hammock, making it swing a little. Otto adjusted, too, using his foot to keep the hammock gently swaying as it cradled the three of them. Ellen called out the back door, saying it was time to go. Cora sighed, and thinking of the long night of writing ahead of her, wriggled out of the hammock and bid Otto and Zoe good night.

TERESA saw Priscilla and Ron to the door when they left. Their son had obviously had a good time, and Ron loosened up considerably over the course of the evening. He'd had a long talk with Gary, which Teresa thought was perfect. Their boys had both struggled in school and there was no question (for everyone but Melissa, of course) that Jacob was doing great.

Others were leaving in dribs and drabs, collecting their plates and packing up their children. Jacob and Melissa had gone home together, but Zoe, whose lemon squares had all been gobbled up, stayed behind with Gary. Lizzie's pie was completely gone, too, and so were the beef empanadas. Carmen had packed up the extra veggie ones and sent them off with Stacy and Sam.

Alice offered to leave the remaining serving of lasagne but Teresa insisted she take it, winking at a smiling Bill as Alice relent-ed. Pina scooped the last serving of mac and cheese into a plastic container so Russell could have it for lunch the following day, and Teresa gave her a container of leftover chili and some guacamole.

"So, it's officially summer," said Carmen, washing her pie plate and platters and putting them in a canvas bag.

"Yup," said Pina. "Who's going to the beach next week?"

"Not sure about us," said Teresa. "Otto starts programming camp, and Vera is volunteering at the library. I think Cora is, too."

"Lizzie is doing the city sailing program," said Carmen.

"Yeah," said Pina, "Anthony and Dominic are doing that, too."

"Oh, there'll be plenty of people at the beach," said Teresa.

Russell had turned on the ball game in the living room and Henry, Lou, and Gary had joined him, Emma asleep on Henry's lap. The rest of the kids could be heard on the front porch, sitting cross legged in a circle and learning a chant that Aria was teaching them, the sounds of their rhythmical claps and pealing laughter floating on the night air, an occasional off the beat clap punctuating the perfection. The women smiled at each other.

"They're having fun," said Carmen.

Teresa poked Pina's ribs and said, "Poor Jewel, you shouldn't have gotten on her case about Rock."

"Somebody has to," said Pina. "And it's true, what I said about forbidden fruit."

"At least Alice didn't bring the dog," said Carmen.

"Mm, hmm," said Teresa, feeling relaxed. She surveyed the kitchen table, thinking clean up could wait until tomorrow. "I wonder if those new people will decide to homeschool."

"Who knows," said Pina.

They were all thinking the same thing, but leave it to Pina to say it. "Our kids are getting so big."

"I know," said Carmen, tearing up.

"Hey," said Teresa, snaking an arm around her. "Come on, it's not over yet."

"Close, though," said Pina. Pina wasn't helping, but Teresa wasn't really worried about Carmen. She knew her well enough to know that her tears would be over momentarily.

They fell quiet, listening to the distant sounds of clapping and chanting from the front porch.

"When do you think they'll start looking for us?" said Carmen.

Pina guffawed. "Never."

Teresa turned to the open back window to check on the fire, and saw that two of the kids were not part of the group chanting on the front porch. Otto and Zoe were in the hammock, sneakered feet stretching toward the heat of the fire, hands entwined. Serenaded by crickets, their two faces glowed in the flickering fire light, enraptured by the hot red embers.

ACKNOWLEDGEMENTS

First and foremost, we wish to thank our families for love, support, and inspiration always.

We are grateful to our readers: Tracy Barsamian Ventola for her enthusiastic vote of confidence and encouragement just when we needed it; Lauren Budd for her incisive and meticulous reading and feedback; Claire Dickson for her thoroughness and honest opinion; Glenn Dickson and Nadia Sladkey for their thoughtful impressions; Amy Faeskorn for being one of our early readers; Jenny Arch for her eagle proofreading eye; and Julie Nathon Sayigh for boldly agreeing to be our very first reader—her fresh eyes and thought provoking questions helped us shape the book.

Julie was there for us at the end as well, tapping into her considerable design talents to create a book cover we love.

Fred and Nadia Sladkey and Anne Sayigh made important, much appreciated contributions.

To all the members of our homeschooling community, thanks for everything.

ABOUT THE AUTHORS

MILVA MCDONALD is the mother of four amazing adult children, all of whom homeschooled for all or most of their child and teenage years. She started homeschooling in 1991, after reading an essay by John Taylor Gatto and realizing school and the PTA weren't for her. For three decades she worked for *The Boston Globe* and boston.com writing and reporting about arts and cultural events in Boston. Other pursuits over the years included running a folk music coffeehouse, organizing countless field trips, facilitating creative writing groups for kids, passing hors d'oeuvres at fancy parties on weekends, and performing in several editions of *The Christmas Revels*. She sings in *The Halalisa Singers* and blogs at apotlucklife.com.

SOPHIA SAYIGH is a librarian and the mother of two adult children, neither of whom went to school until college. She is forever grateful for the time she was able to spend with them unschooling, and she continues to learn more from each of them than she ever taught them. She stumbled upon John Holt's *Teach Your Own* at the library in 1991, and it struck a deep chord, resonating with her own school experience as a "good" student, as well as her then life with a toddler. She is the ultimate homebody, and has supported families through volunteer work as a breastfeeding counselor, contributing homeschool support group member, and family death care/green burial outreach. A perfect moment would be spent outside in lively conversation with family and friends, a cup of coffee, book, and dog within reach.

TWENTY years ago, Milva and Sophia met through a homeschooling support group and began a long friendship. Together with other families in their homeschooling world, they laughed, hiked, biked, camped, read books, visited museums, and hosted many potlucks. While the kids played, they engaged in fierce discussions about learning, parenting, politics, and education. In 2003, they co-founded a statewide homeschooling non-profit, Advocates for

Home Education in Massachusetts, Inc., to help other families who choose this path. *Unschoolers* is a fictionalized account of their experience as homeschoolers, of the kinds of relationships they enjoyed and witnessed, and the way of life they loved.

47532887R00106

Made in the USA
San Bernardino, CA
01 April 2017